"The monkey has my fire engine!" cried Freddie.

The Bobbsey Twins at Cherry Corners

The Bobbsey Twins at Cherry Corners

BY

LAURA LEE HOPE

AUTHOR OF "THE BOBBSEY TWINS SERIES," "THE BUNNY BROWN SERIES," "THE SIX LITTLE BUNKERS SERIES," "THE OUTDOOR GIRLS SERIES," ETC.

NEW YORK
GROSSET & DUNLAP
PUBLISHERS

Made in the United States of America

The Bobbsey Twins at Cherry Corners

CONTENTS

THE BOBBSEY TWINS AT CHERRY CORNERS

CHAPTER I

THE THIRD ACT

"EVERYTHING is ready now!" called Bert Bobbsey. "Hurry there, Nan. The audience is waiting!"

"I'm coming as fast as I can!" answered Bert's twin sister. "But I have to get Flossie and Freddie. They're in the show, you know."

"Of course!" agreed Bert as he held open the side door of the big garage.

The garage, being empty for the afternoon, was to be used by the twins for giving a "show," to which all the neighborhood children had been invited.

"You couldn't keep Flossie and Freddie

out of this theater if you tied them!" went on Bert. "But we've got to hurry. What's Freddie doing?"

"Oh, he's gone back to the house after his toy fire engine," Nan answered, shaking her dark-brown hair out of her eyes. "He says he wants to be a fireman on the stage."

"I guess we'll have to let him, then," agreed Bert. "But I wish he'd hurry. He's holding the show back. Where's Flossie?"

"Here she comes, and look at her doll! Hasn't she got it dressed cute?"

"Oh, I guess so," answered Bert, who, as manager of the little show, as well as one of the actors in it, had a great many worries—or at least he thought he had. "Come on, Freddie! Hurry!" he called.

At the sound of his voice, in tones louder than he had before used, there was a murmur on the other side of the curtain, which was made of automobile robes and bed comfortables fastened together with safety pins.

The curtain hung from the edge of a loft which extended halfway across the garage at the rear. It really was a second story.

but there was only half a floor, which was reached by an open stairway.

The curtain of this improvised theater had a heavy pole fastened to the bottom. It was a round pole which had formed the center roll of a new rug Mrs. Bobbsey had bought. The upper edge of the curtain was nailed to the edge of the loft. By pulling on ropes at either end of the round pole, ropes which went over small pulleys, the curtain could be raised and lowered, making the garage seem very like a real show house.

"I'm coming, Bert!" Freddie called from the garden path, as he came hurrying along, clasping in his arms a small fire engine, which, though a toy, spurted out real water when the spring of the pump was wound up. "I'm going to be a fireman in the play," he added.

"But you were supposed to be a cowboy, Freddie," objected Nan, who had helped Bert put the little play together.

"I'm going to be a fireman!" the little boy insisted. From the time Freddie Bobbsey was a very little fellow he had played at putting out fires. So much so that his father often called him "little fireman," just as he called Flossie his "fat fairy," for the other small twin used often to pretend that she was a little elf.

"Look here now," began Bert rather seriously, as Freddie came through the side door—the "stage entrance," so to speak. "You can't go spoiling things this way, Freddie Bobbsey! You said you wanted to be a cowboy and I went ahead and fixed the play that way. Now you want to be a fireman. You can't do things like that!"

"I'm going to be a fireman!" insisted Freddie sweetly enough, but quite firmly. "I have my fire engine and I'm going to be a fireman!"

"Oh, huckleberries!" cried Bert, waving his hands. "If you go on like this——"

"Let him be a cowboy-fireman," broke in Nan, anxious for peace. "How would that do?"

"Oh, yes, I'd like to be a cowboy-fireman!" exclaimed Freddie.

"All right—go ahead then," agreed Bert. "But we can't make any changes now. We have to get dressed and the play's got to start The audience will get tired of waiting."

This seemed to be very true, for from the other side of the curtain where the neighborhood boys and girls, seated on boxes, barrels, and planks, were anticipating what was to follow, came calls of:

"Hurry up!"

"Start the show!"

"When are they going to begin?"

"Pull up the curtain!"

"Yes, we have to hurry!" decided Nan. "Come in here, Flossie, and I'll help you get dressed."

"I can dress myself," said Freddie to Bert.

"You'll have to," was the answer of the older lad. "I'll have all I can do to get ready in time. Don't open that door!" he called in a loud whisper to Nan, who had walked toward a closet.

"Why not?" the brown-haired girl asked.

"Snoop and Snap are locked in there. They're going to be in the show, and if you open that door now they'll run out."

"Then I won't open it," promised Nan, for well she knew how eager the cat and the dog would be to get away from the noise and confusion of the play.

"They're going on in the last act," explained Bert.

The four actors talked in whispers, for the "theater" was so small and the stage was so close to the audience on the other side of the curtain that nearly everything said in an ordinary voice could be heard "out front."

Then began a busy time. Nan had her own costume to put on, in addition to helping her small sister get ready. Bert had to attire himself as a pirate, while Freddie, in his dual rôle of a fireman and a cowboy, was getting into a strange mixture of clothes.

"What kind of a hat does a cowboy-fireman wear, Bert?" asked Freddie. "I have a regular cowboy hat, but a fireman's is different."

"Oh, I have troubles of my own!" sighed Bert. "Wear it any way you like."

"Here, Freddie," called Nan, who saw the worried look on her small brother's face. "I'll fix it for you."

This she did by pinning the cowboy hat up in the front and turning it down in the back somewhat like a fireman's helmet, yet still preserving some looks of a sombrero.

The "play," which Bert and Nan had arranged between themselves, was really very simple. The first act opened on a "ship," which Bert had made with a lot of packing boxes, some boards, and a bed sheet tied around a clothesline prop for a sail and a mast. In the opening scene Bert was supposed to be a lone pirate, walking the deck of his vessel.

Then he pretended to see a raft floating on the water, and on the raft were Flossie and Nan, who had been set adrift when their ship went down. Bert was to stop his ship and rescue the two from the raft, and they were to come up on deck.

"Then we'll have some songs," Bert had said. "I'll sing a pirate's song, and you can sing some other song, Nan."

"Can't I sing?" Flossie had asked. "I know a lovely song about a little lamb and a bird and a bee."

"Pirates don't like songs about lambs and birds!" Bert had declared.

"Oh, let her sing it!" Nan had pleaded, and Bert had agreed, on condition that Nan would sing a song begging her pirate captor to set her free. Consequently, Nan had made up such a ditty.

The second act of the play was to represent the pirate and his captives on a desert island around a campfire (Mr. Bobbsey had insisted, of course, that the fire be only a make-believe one) and Freddie, as a cowboy, was to rescue Flossie and Nan. But the plot had been complicated by Freddie's insisting on being a fireman as well as a cowboy.

"We can let him put out the pirate campfire," Nan whispered to Bert.

"All right! Only hurry up!" the stage manager begged in a hoarse whisper. "Hear 'em clapping out there?"

Indeed the audience seemed to be getting impatient, as well they might, for they had come to be amused and matters were being delayed.

At last all was in readiness. Back of the curtain some homemade properties had been set about to represent the deck of a ship—coils of rope, the clothesline, two tubs, an old spinning wheel for the steering wheel of the craft, and other things.

"Pull up the curtain!" shrilly whispered

Bert, and he and Nan, taking hold of ropes on either side of the stage, hauled away, rolling up the comfortables and the auto robes. This disclosed the "ship's deck," and amid the clapping of hands Bert, now as the pirate actor, strode across it.

"'Tis a gay life to be a pirate!" cried Bert, waving his wooden sword, stained with blackberry juice. "But 'tis sad at times. Where are all my brave men? Sunk! Sunk!" And so he recited on, really doing very well. Suddenly he seemed to see something afloat on the heaving ocean. He put his hand to his eyes, in true pirate fashion, and shouted:

"Raft ahoy! Where away! By the mainmast, 'tis a lone maiden!"

Then Bert began to sing a song, which was loudly applauded at the finish. A moment later Nan and Flossie came over the side, begging to be saved. The two little girls fell on their knees and sang a duet.

This, also, was applauded, and then Nan and Bert sang together, which seemed to please the audience. After that Flossie sang alone, carrying her doll, and she was so funny that she had to give an encore. When Nan told her in a whisper to give an encore, Flossie did not know what was meant until Bert said:

"Go on and do it again!"

The first act went off very well, but the closing scene was nearly spoiled when Freddie thrust his head out from behind a pile of boxes that represented the ship cabin and hoarsely whispered:

"Hey, Bert! When does my turn come?"

The curtain on the first act was let down amid tumultuous clapping of hands, stamping of feet on the garage floor, and cries of:

"Good! Good! That's fine!"

"Now we have to get ready for the second act!" said Bert who, from being the chief actor in the rôle of pirate, now became the stage manager. "Hurry up, everybody. We have to set the island scene up now."

"That's where I put out the fire, don't I?" asked Freddie.

"Yes. But hush, dear," begged Nan. "They'll hear you out in front."

There was much scurrying about back of the curtain, and, after a while, the stage was set to look something like an island. This scene was really quite effective, since Nan and Bert had planted tree branches and bushes in boxes of earth, and when these were placed around the rear of the garage the place looked quite like a bit of nature. Of course there was no water.

"But I have some in my fire engine," Freddie said.

Up went the curtain again, and the audience applauded the scene before the actors said a word. But the talk soon started. Flossie and Nan planned to escape from the clutches of the pirate, who was stalking moodily about the campfire, sighing for more ships to capture.

Again there was singing by the two sets of twins, for Freddie was on in this scene as a cowboy-fireman, and managed to get through some verses his mother had taught him.

Since the use of the toy fire engine had not been planned when Bert got up his play, that versatile character had to make some quick changes. It was decided that Flossie and Nan were to steal away in the night, and to this end Freddie was to put out the campfire with his engine. This pleased the little chap mightily.

In due time, after several songs, the pirate chief went to sleep beside the fire—make-believe, of course. Then Freddie came stalking on with his toy engine filled with water.

"Here is one who will help us escape!" whispered Nan to Flossie, who was supposed to be sleeping beside her. "Here comes a brave cowboy."

"And fireman, too! I'm a fireman!" added Freddie in a whisper. "Say I'm a fireman, too!"

There were some laughs from the audience, but Nan added:

"This brave cowboy-fireman will save us. But 'tis too light. The fire will show our movements to the pirate!"

"Have no fear!" declaimed Freddie. "I will put out the fire!' This he proceeded to do, starting the toy engine which pumped a real stream of water. By mistake Freddie squirted some in Bert's face, though to the credit of that actor be it said he never moved, but slept on.

"Fire's out!" cried Freddie. "Come on,

Nan!" There was another laugh from the audience at this "break," but no one minded, and the curtain came down on the second act amid loud applause.

"The third act ends with Snoop and Snap doing some of their tricks," Bert explained to his fellow workers and helpers.

"I guess they'll be glad to get out of the closet," added Nan.

The third act began well, with the actors in fine form. This scene was on a raft after the pirate had been taken captive by Nan, Flossie, and Freddie. Bert was bound with ropes to the raft's mast.

On board were Snap and Snoop, who were supposed to have been taken away from the desert island. To bring things about naturally, Nan was to say:

"This is a long, lonely voyage. Let us be amused. Perhaps this dog and cat can do some tricks?"

"They will do tricks for me, fair maiden, if you will unbind me," Bert remarked in pirate tones.

"Will you promise not to hurt us if we unbind thee?" Nan asked.

"I promise, lady fair!"

The ropes were then cast off Bert who, having trained Snap and Snoop, knew how to put them through their paces. He had his pets do some simple tricks, to the delight of the audience, and the third act was coming to a beautiful close, with the two animals chasing Bert around the stage, when there was a rumbling, bumping noise in the loft overhead.

"Oh, what's that?" cried Flossie.

"Never mind!" hoarsely whispered Bert. "Keep still! Don't spoil the scene. This is the climax!"

But the climax came in different fashion than was expected. Suddenly, the curtain fell down with a crash, the pole bumping on the floor. Then followed a succession of rumbling, bumping sounds, while the audience began a mad scramble to escape.

CHAPTER II

MOTHER'S NEWS

"WHAT'S happening?" screamed some of the children in the audience.

"The garage is coming down!" exclaimed Danny Rugg, always an excitable chap.

"Let me get out!" begged Grace Lavine.

"There's no danger! No danger at all!" yelled Bert. "Nobody will get hurt!"

But Snap, the dog, was barking, and Snoop, his tail as big as a bologna sausage, was scrambling off the "raft." Flossie and Freddie did not know what to make of the strange racket and the sudden fall of the curtain.

"It's all right. No danger at all!" cried John Marsh, who was one of Bert's particular chums.

"What happened?" asked Helen Porter.

"A lot of baskets of potatoes fell down off

that place," and John pointed to the loft over the stage. "That's all it is—a lot of potatoes falling down."

By this time the audience and the players could see that it was this that had happened. Potatoes were rolling all about the floor and across what had been the stage.

"Did you do that, Sammie Todd?" demanded Nan Bobbsey, for, be it known, Sam was a mischievous lad, always up to some trick.

"I did not! I wasn't out of my seat!" he replied.

"That's right. Sammie was sitting next to me," chimed in Danny Rugg, but some of the girls were heard to murmur that it would be "just like" those two boys to do something like this.

"Well, the play's over," remarked Bert somewhat sadly, for the curtain had collapsed, the fastenings having pulled away. It would take some time to put it in place again. Moreover, some of those who had been on the pirate raft were gone. Snoop and Snap had run out of the garage.

Potatoes were scattered about everywhere,

amid the overturned chairs, boxes, benches, and planks on which the audience had been seated. The scenery of the stage was all disarranged. The play was ruined—wrecked —spoiled!

"Never mind—it was almost over, anyhow," said Nan to Bert.

"Yes, it was almost over. But look at the mess we'll have to clean up now," and he sighed. "I wonder how it happened," he went on, musingly.

While Bert is wondering and while the excitement is calming down, I will take just a moment to tell new readers something about the Bobbsey twins and their friends.

There were two sets of them, as you have seen. Flossie and Freddie were the younger twins.. They had light hair and blue eyes. Bert and Nan, who were some years older than the others, had brown hair and brown eyes.

In the book, "The Bobbsey Twins," these four children were first introduced. They lived with their father and mother, Mr. and Mrs. Richard Bobbsey, in the eastern city of Lakeport, on Lake Metoka, on the shore of which Mr. Bobbsey owned a lumberyard.

With the family also lived Sam Johnson, a colored man of all work, and his wife Dinah, who was the cook. In a way, Snap, the dog, and Snoop, the cat, were also members of the family, for the children liked their pets very much.

Bert and Nan, as well as Flossie and Freddie, had wonderfully good times at their home, in the country on grandpa's farm, at school, and going about to different places when the summer vacation closed their classes. Their adventures you will find set down in various books.

Just before the opening of this story the children had taken part in some queer happenings, as related in the volume entitled "The Bobbsey Twins at Cloverbank." They had returned from there to their home, and now, with summer coming on again, Bert and his sisters and brother were ready for more fun. It had been Bert's idea to get up the play in the garage.

"But I never thought it would end this way," he said a bit ruefully, as he looked at the scattered things on the garage floor.

"We'll help you clean up," offered Charlie Mason.

"Sure!" echoed Danny Rugg. "It was a good show until the curtain smashed down on that third act."

"And then it wasn't so very bad!" chuckled the fun-loving Sammie. "I thought it was all part of the play when I saw those potatoes tumbling down like a queer kind of rain."

"I wonder what made them fall!" said Bert again. "I'm going to have a look."

"Didn't you know they were up there?" asked Charlie.

"No, I didn't. I saw a lot of baskets up there, but I didn't know they had potatoes in 'em."

But that is what the baskets held, and it turned out that Sam Johnson had stored the potatoes in the garage loft. Bert had not fastened the heavy curtain very securely, and it was found that, unknowingly, he had tied some of the supporting ropes around the potato baskets.

The raising and lowering of the curtain had shifted these baskets, until some toppled over.

knocking others down, and then had come the grand crash.

No one was hurt. Snoop and Snap were the ones most frightened, and they scampered away. A few of the girls had run outside, but they soon came back, and while some helped Nan pick up the scattered clothes that had served as costumes in the play others assisted the boys to gather the potatoes.

"I didn't know there were this many potatoes in the world!" exclaimed Charlie Mason.

"Pooh! You ought to see how many my grandfather digs on his farm!" said Bert.

But if the audience and actors in the pirate play were soon over their excitement caused by the fall of the potatoes and the curtain, Dinah, the fat, good-natured colored cook, did not share this freedom from worry.

She had paused in the midst of baking a cake long enough to ask her husband, Sam, who was cutting the lawn:

"Whar am de chilluns?"

"Dem's all in de garage play-actin'," Sam had replied, and Dinah had assumed that Bert and the others were all right. She heard laughter and applause coming from the "theater," and smiled and chuckled as she murmured:

"Bress der h'a'ts. Dey's havin' oceans ob fun!"

Then had sounded the wild shouts and cries, the crash, and many bumping noises.

"Good lan' ob massy!" yelled Dinah, dropping on the table the cake she had just taken from the oven. "Dey mus' be some conglomeration out dere! Oh, I hope de chillums ain't hurted!"

She rushed from the house just as Mr. and Mrs. Bobbsey, who had been out riding in the automobile, turned into the drive. Mrs. Bobbsey, seeing Dinah running frantically, at once guessed that something was wrong. Dinah was like a watchdog with the children.

"What is it?" cried Mrs. Bobbsey, as her husband stopped the car.

"Sumpin done happened!" gasped Dinah. "De honey lambs am out in de garage, but dey's a conglomeration out dere, I guess! Heah 'em!"

Indeed, the two parents could not very well help hearing the commotion. For a moment Mr. Bobbsey, as did his wife, feared something dreadful had happened, and they hurried toward the "theater." They soon heard laughter replacing the cries of alarm and saw such of the audience as had run out going back in, so they felt relieved.

"I guess it's only part of the play," chuckled Mr. Bobbsey as he turned about to go back and shut off the motor of the car, which had been left going.

But Mrs. Bobbsey wanted to make sure, so she continued on to the garage, entering it in time to see the children picking up the potatoes.

"Is dey all killed?" gasped Dinah, who was afraid to look.

"Nonsense! They're all right!" laughed Mrs. Bobbsey. "What happened, Bert?" she asked.

"Curtain fell down and pulled with it a lot of potatoes Sam had stored in the loft," was the boy's explanation.

"Oh, Mother! We had a fine play until that happened!" said Flossie. "I was on a pirate raft."

"And I was a cowboy-fireman," added Freddie.

"Too bad your play had to be spoiled," said the children's mother.

"Oh, it wasn't exactly spoiled," admitted Bert. "It didn't happen until near the end of the third act, and that was the last. But it sure did make a racket!"

"I was frightened!" admitted Nan.

"Well, don't worry about it," advised Mrs. Bobbsey. "You were only going to give one performance, anyhow. And now there is something else to look forward to."

"Oh, what, Mother?" cried Nan, impressed by something in her mother's voice and by a light shining in Mrs. Bobbsey's eyes. "Is it a secret?"

"No, not exactly a secret," was the laughing answer. "As soon as you finish cleaning up, come into the house, twins, and I'll tell you the news!"

"Oh, hurray! We're going somewhere, I'm almost sure!" shouted Bert, as he tossed the scattered potatoes into a basket.

CHAPTER III

DINAH'S APPLE CART

WITH the work of cleaning up the mess well under way, Mrs. Bobbsey turned back toward the house, to observe Dinah standing a little distance from the garage.

"Am dey—am dey much hurted?" asked the faithful old cook.

"Nonsense, Dinah! No one is hurt at all!" answered the children's mother. "It was just a small accident—some potatoes were spilled and the curtain crashed down. No one was hurt."

"Dat's good!" sighed Dinah. "But dat dere dog an' cat—dey was scairt, I reckon! Yo' should 'a' seen 'em run out!" and she chuckled.

"Yes, I suppose Snap and Snoop were a bit frightened," agreed Mrs. Bobbsey. "But they'll soon get over it."

Not all the boys and girls that had made up the audience at the pirate play remained to help clean up things. Most of them drifted off after a few half-hearted efforts to assist to find other fun. But Charlie Mason and John Marsh, two of Bert's particular chums, remained to help with the potatoes.

"Are you folks going away?" asked John, who had overheard some of the talk between Bert and his mother.

"I guess so," was the answer. "We go away every summer vacation. But up to now nothing has been said about where we are going."

"I hope we go to the seashore!" exclaimed Freddie. "There's lots of water for my fire engine!"

"Oh, you and your fire engine!" laughed Nan, giving him a little hug as she held out a basket so he could put in it some potatoes he had picked up.

"I'd rather go to the mountains," chimed in Flossie. "It's better air up there for my dolls, and my best one is sick."

"Yes, the mountains are nice," agreed Nan.

"I'd like to go to a farm," Bert said.

"That's the best place of all!" agreed Charlie. "We're going on a farm this summer."

"We're going to the seashore," said John. "It's the first time, and I hope I'll like it."

"You'll be sure to," said Bert, and then they began talking of the different kinds of fun to be had during the long vacation.

But through it all Bert was wondering what his mother had to tell him and the other twins. He knew she and his father had ridden off to a distant city on business. It was because the automobile was to be out of the garage that the play had been planned for this day.

"I wonder what Mother will tell us?" murmured Nan to Bert, when most of the potatoes had been picked up.

"We'll find out in a little while," he answered. "Do you think our play was all right, Nan?"

"It was fine—all but the last curtain!" and she laughed merrily, as did Charlie and John.

"Maybe we'll have another some day—

when we get back in the fall," Bert half promised, as his chums drifted off to the street.

"Well, children," began Mrs. Bobbsey when, a little later, the four twins went up to where she was sitting on a side porch, "are you all right?"

"All right, Mother," answered Bert. "But what's the news?"

"Tell us where we are going this summer!" begged Nan.

"Did I say we were going anywhere?" teased Mrs. Bobbsey. "How would it be if we stayed at home this summer?"

"Oh, Mother!" came in disappointed tones from all four, and Freddie and Flossie looked so distressed that their father, who had come up the steps, laughed and said:

"I guess we'd better tell them and have it over with, Mother!"

"All right!" agreed his wife. "Then, children, this is what we are going to do. In a week we are going to Cherry Corners!"

"Cherry Corners?" echoed Nan and Bert.

"Where is Cherry Corners?" Flossie wanted to know.

"Is there any water there for my fire engine?" demanded Freddie.

"Plenty!" chuckled his father. "But you are getting to be a poor shot with that hose of yours, my little fireman."

"A poor shot?" repeated Freddie, in wonderment.

"Yes," and his father laughed harder than ever. "I hear that when you tried to put out the pirate's fire you squirted water in Bert's ear!"

"That's what he did!" chuckled Bert. "I had all I could do not to yell out and spoil the scene. You ought to feel that water tickle!"

"I—I—now—couldn't help it!" stammered Freddie. "But I squirted only a little on Bert."

"Who told you about it, Daddy?" asked Nan.

"Charlie Mason," answered Mr. Bobbsey. "I was just talking to him out in the street. Oh, well, what matter? You had a good time," and the Bobbsey twins agreed that they certainly had.

"But what about Cherry Corners?" asked Nan. "What is it and where is it?"

"Is it on a farm?" Bert wanted to know.

"Yes, it's on four farms," his father replied. "Or rather, there are four farms at Cherry Corners. Four farms meet at the crossroads, and on each farm are a number of cherry trees. Cherries will soon be ripe and——"

"Are we going up there in time to pick cherries?" asked Flossie eagerly.

"I love cherries!" chimed in Freddie.

"And cherry pie," added Bert. "Oh, boy!"

"What about it, Mother?" asked Nan, for the vital question had not yet been answered.

"Yes, we are planning to take you to Cherry Corners this summer," said Mrs. Bobbsey. "Your father will tell you about it. I must go in to tell Dinah about dinner."

As Mrs. Bobbsey entered the house, the four twins turned to their father with eager faces.

"This is how it happened," went on Mr. Bobbsey, who liked to explain matters to his children so they would understand just how things came about. "Cherry Corners is the name of a country town about seventy-five miles from here. The place is named after four farms containing many cherry trees.

"Now, it so came about that a certain man who owned one of these farms bought a lot of lumber from me to build some houses in another town. He thought he could make more money building houses than he could working on his farm and selling cherries. So I let him have the lumber and he promised either to pay me later or give me his farm if he could not pay in money.

"Well, things did not turn out so well in his building work, and now he wants me to take the farm in payment for the lumber I gave him. That is only fair."

"Are you going to take the farm, Daddy?" asked Bert.

"Yes, it seems the only thing to do. I don't exactly want a farm, for I have little time to work on it. But since I had to take it, I thought you and your mother might as well have a nice vacation on it. This farm is the best of the four, and has the most cherry trees on it."

"But are there cherries on the trees, Daddy?" asked Flossie.

"Lots of them!" laughed her father. "In fact, your mother and I just now got back from having visited this farm, which is called Red Gate, because the entrance has a big red gate. The cherries will soon be ripe—I should say in another week or two."

"May we pick as many as we like?" asked Freddie.

"Yes," his father answered, and then he shook his finger warningly at not only the little "fireman" twin, but at the other three as well.

"What is it, Daddy?" asked Nan.

"You may pick as many cherries as you like," said Mr. Bobbsey a bit solemnly, "but you may not eat as many as you like. I don't mean that all the fruit has to be sold," he went on. "But you must not eat so many cherries as to make youselves ill. Be careful and wise—that is what you must do if you go to Cherry Corners."

"We will!" promised Bert for the others. "Are there cows and horses and pigs and chickens and all things like that on the farm?"

"Some of these things are on Red Gate,

and some on the other farms around there," Mr. Bobbsey explained. "It's a regular country place, if that's what you mean."

"That's what I mean," said Bert. "Oh, what fun we'll have!"

"What fun! What fun!" echoed the other twins.

Freddie jumped off the porch and began to run around, joyfully singing, and Flossie was just going to join him when Freddie took it into his head to run down the path and up the back steps, calling to Flossie:

"You can't catch me!"

Just as he started up the back steps Dinah started down with a bowl of custard in her hands, intending to set it outside to cool a bit before putting it in the refrigerator. A moment later Freddie crashed full tilt into the black cook, scattering the custard all over. Dinah caught her breath, then cried:

"Good lan' ob massy! He's done upsot mah apple cart!"

CHAPTER IV

SCATTERED BERRIES

DINAH did not have an apple cart, of course. She just called her jolly, fat body that in fun. But Freddie, in his excited running race to celebrate the news about going to Cherry Corners, had certainly knocked Dinah down and had spilled the bowl of custard.

"Oh! Oh!" gasped Flossie, as, with horrified eyes, she saw what her brother had done. "Oh, Freddie Bobbsey!"

Dinah, who had sat down, and rather hard, too, if the truth is to be told, said nothing after her first cry. One reason for this was that there was a lot of custard in her mouth and on her face and on her dress.

There was also custard on Freddie's face,

and so much around his mouth that the little fellow could only exclaim:

"Glub! Wob! Ulp!"

Then, with a quick motion of his hand, he wiped some of the egg, milk, and sugar off his face and managed to gasp:

"I—I—I didn't mean to do it, Dinah!"

"Bress yo' h'a't, honey lamb, I known yo' didn't!" declared Dinah, and then her fat body began to shake like a bowl of jelly, for she was laughing.

"Freddie!" called his mother in shocked surprise, "what did you do a thing like that for?"

"I—I didn't mean to," said the little fellow again.

"Are you hurt, Dinah?" asked Mr. Bobbsey, as he hastened forward to pick up the cook.

"Oh, no, sah, I isn't hurt!" she answered. "I's jest shook up a bit, but dat's all. De custard is done spoiled, dough."

"There isn't any of it left," observed Bert, trying not to laugh. "We might scrape some off Dinah and Freddie, though."

No one seemed to think this idea a very

good one, and while Dinah got up off the ground and found the bowl, which luckily was not broken, Freddie was picked up by his mother and carried into the house to be washed and have clean clothes laid out for him.

"I guess I'll have to change mah dress," murmured Dinah. "An' dere ain't time fo' no mo' custard makin' I reckon."

"Don't think of it, Dinah," advised Mrs. Bobbsey. "We'll have something else for dessert. How did you happen to run into Dinah, Freddie?"

"Oh, I just did it—that's all," was his answer.

"He was excited about Cherry Corners," declared Nan.

"Mustn't get too excited," warned Mr. Bobbsey. "You might fall out of cherry trees while you're gathering the fruit. Now calm down. This has been rather an exciting day."

So it had been, starting with the play, the accident when the curtain came down, spilling the potatoes, and now the upsetting of Dinah and the bowl of custard.

But that brought the mishaps to an end, and in the evening after dinner the children sat about and talked quietly of what they would do when they got to Cherry Corners.

"Are we going by train, Daddy?" asked Flossie, who dearly loved to travel this way.

But this time the Bobbsey twins were not to go by train, as their father soon informed them. In answer to Flossie's question he stated:

"We will go to Red Gate Farm, at Cherry Corners, in our auto. It will be a trip of only about three hours."

"Can I take my fire engine in the auto?" Freddie asked.

"And my dolls?" added Flossie.

"If we all go in the auto, and those twins take all the toys they want, there won't be any room for trunks," said Bert, who was a practical boy.

"The trunks will go by express, on the train," said his father.

"Then there'll be plenty of room," observed Nan, for the Bobbsey auto was a large touring car.

The next day the four twins told some of their playmates about the good times in store for them, and more than one boy or girl who lived near the Bobbsey home murmured:

"I wish I were going to Cherry Corners!'

As a matter of fact, most of them were going to different, jolly vacation places, and they all counted on having good times. But none of them thought he or she was going to such a wonderful spot as Cherry Corners seemed to be.

"I hope it's as nice as Daddy and Mother say it is," said Nan to Bert, when they were talking it over later in the day.

"Oh, I guess it will be," the boy answered. "There's a small river up at Red Gate Dad said, and I'm going fishing."

A voice at the gate called to Nan, and she saw Helen Porter coming up the walk.

"Don't you want to come with me?" asked Helen, who had a basket on her arm.

"Where are you going?" asked Nan.

"To take some things to Mrs. Clockford. Mother always sends her a basket of food each week."

"Oh, isn't that lovely!" exclaimed Nan.

who knew about the poor widow who lived at the other end of the street on which stood the Bobbsey and Porter homes. "Wait, I'll ask Dinah if I can take her some. Mother isn't at home, but it will be all right if Dinah gives me a basket."

When the colored cook heard of the girls' errand of mercy, she filled a basket for Nan, so that the two children started off, well laden, to call on Mrs. Clockford.

"Oh, wait a minute!" exclaimed Nan, when she was at the gate. "I forgot something."

"You have your hat," Helen reminded her playmate.

"Oh, it isn't that," laughed Nan. "It's about Flossie and Freddie. Mother has gone down town shopping, and she told me to watch them. If I go away, those twins are sure to get into mischief."

"There's Bert," said Helen, pointing to Nan's other brother, who was oiling his bicycle in the front yard.

"He won't be around here long," Nan replied. "He's going off on his wheel. Let me see—what can I do? We can't take them with us, and Dinah is too busy to watch them. Bert won't be here and——"

Just then Flossie and Freddie came running around the corner of the house with Henry and Mary Blackburn, two neighboring children about their own age.

"Oh, Nan!" called Flossie, "may Freddie and I go over to Mary's house to play?"

"Did your mother say it would be all right, Mary?" Nan asked the visitor.

"Oh, yes," was the ready answer. "Henry and I came over to get Flossie and Freddie. Mother sent us, and she said she'd watch to see that nothing happened."

"Then it will be all right," decided Nan, with a sigh of relief. "I can go with you, Helen."

"I'm so glad!" murmured the other girl. "Poor Mrs. Clockford doesn't have much to eat. She likes company, too. I always stay and talk with her a little while."

"Then I will, too," agreed Nan.

She heard the laughter of Flossie and Freddie as they scurried across the yards toward the home of their playmates.

"I'm going, Bert," Nan called to the elder

Bobbsey lad. "Tell Mother, when she comes back, that I won't be very long."

"All right—I will if I'm here!" sang out Bert. "But I'm going for a bike ride and I don't know when I'm coming home. I'm going to get my wheel in shape to take to Cherry Corners."

"Bert's a good rider, isn't he?" asked Helen as she and Nan started off down the street, carrying the baskets of food.

"He thinks he is!" laughed Nan. "But he fell off once, though when I remind him of it he says he did it on purpose."

"I guess he can ride all right," decided Helen. "But tell me about Cherry Corners. It sounds like a beautiful place."

"I guess it is, but I've never been there," answered Nan. "I'll send you a picture postcard of it if I can find one after we get there."

Talking of many things and promising to write to each other during their vacation, Nan and Helen went on their way. Meanwhile Bert, having finished oiling his wheel, prepared to set out on it to visit John Marsh, his chum who lived several blocks away.

John had two fishing rods and outfits, and had said he might trade one to Bert for a pair of roller skates that Bert no longer cared about.

"My fish pole is getting old," Bert decided. "If I could get that extra one of John's for my old roller skates, it would be just the thing."

He hung the skates by their straps over his handle bars, and then trundled his wheel out the front gate and was soon on his way. The sun was shining, the sky was blue, and altogether the weather was just what it should be when school had closed for the long vacation.

Bert rode along several streets, keeping close to the curb of the different highways so as to be out of the path of automobiles as he had been told to do. He was whistling merrily, for there seemed happy times in prospect.

Just before he reached the street on which John lived, Bert saw a wagon, drawn by a bony horse, moving slowly along ahead of him. On one side of the wagon was a man who was shouting loudly:

"Berries! Berries! Here y'are! Nice, fresh blackberries!"

On the other side of the wagon was a boy about Bert's age, but a bit larger and heavier. He, too, carried several boxes of berries and was shouting like the man.

Bert decided to go to the left, which was the rule of the road in passing another vehicle going in the same direction as himself, and he thought he would thus be in no danger should the bony horse suddenly turn in toward the curb, as might happen if some woman called to the man that she wanted berries.

Just as Bert came opposite the boy, the latter, who was walking forward, suddenly began to walk backward. Why he did this Bert could not guess, unless he was too lazy to turn around. But the fact remains that the strange boy, carrying perhaps ten boxes of blackberries on a sort of wooden tray, was going backward. Bert was not going fast, but he was pedaling along a bit too speedily to make a sudden stop. So when he was close to the backward-walking boy and saw what was likely to happen, the Bobbsey lad shouted:

"Hey! Look out!"

But just then the boy was trying to shout as loudly as the man did, and yelled:

"Berries! Berries! Here y'are! Nice blackberries!"

Bert back-pedaled and thus put on his brake, but not in time. He yelled again, but it was too late.

A moment later he ran full tilt into the boy's back and sent him sprawling into the street, scattering the boxes of berries all about. At the same time Bert toppled off his wheel, which clattered to the asphalt, and he fell close beside the boy, sitting down hard on one of the boxes of blackberries.

CHAPTER V

AN ANGRY PEDDLER

BERT BOBBSEY was as much surprised at what had happened as was the peddler's boy. Up to almost the last moment Bert had hoped he might avoid the accident by steering to one side. But the other boy had backed quickly, his two legs had fairly straddled the front wheel of the bicycle, and then had followed the upset.

"Hi there! What's the matter?" yelled the peddler's boy, as he scrambled to his feet and looked around. All that he held of what had been several quarts of berries was the wooden tray on which the boxes had rested. The berries were scattered around the street and some of the boxes were crushed, either by the weight of the boys' bodies or by the bicycle.

"I couldn't help it!" declared Bert, as he also prepared to rise. "You backed right into me. I yelled to you!"

"You did not!" declared the other boy in angry, snarling tones. "You bumped into me on purpose, and I'll fix you for it, see!"

"It was an accident!" exclaimed Bert, getting ready to defend himself, for it seemed as if the other fellow were going to hit him. "You walked backward, and you know it. And I yelled, but you were hollering so loud you couldn't hear me."

"Well, I have a right to holler, ain't I?" demanded the other, who was scowling. Bert noticed that his clothes were ragged and that he was a tall, strong lad. In a fight he might easily get the better of the Bobbsey lad.

By this time the man peddler came around from the other side of his wagon, the horse of which had stopped.

"What's the matter" he asked in a husky voice. Then, when he saw the scattered berries and the broken boxes together with the fallen bicycle, he went on: "Here's a nasty mess! Who did this? Some more of your carelessness, Nick Dodge! Well, you'll pay for them smashed berries! I'll take it out of your wages! My! My! Ten quarts mashed!"

"It wasn't my fault!" declared the ragged helper whose name seemed to be Nick Dodge. "He ran into me!" and he pointed to Bert.

"That's not true!" exclaimed Bert earnestly. "He backed up—backed right toward me, and he kept on backing after I yelled at him to stop. I tried to steer out of his way, but he backed right up on my wheel. It wasn't my fault."

"What were you backing up for, Nick Dodge?" demanded the peddler.

"I wasn't!" insisted the other. "He ran plumb into me. And I'll make him pay for those berries, too!" Nick yelled in sudden rage as he leaped forward and grabbed Bert's arm.

"Let me alone!" shouted Bert, pulling away and getting ready to clench his fists and fight, if need be.

At this moment two men who had been walking on the sidewalk stepped into the street, and one called to Nick:

"Let go that kid's arm! It was your fault!"

"That's right!" added the other man. "Just as he says, young peddler, you were backing. We heard him shout to you!"

"Well, I didn't hear him," asserted Nick as, reluctantly enough, he let go of Bert's arm. "He ran into me all right!"

"Because you were walking backward," said one of the men who had taken Bert's part. "That's no way to do in the middle of the street. An auto might hit you."

"What in the world were you walking backward for?" asked Hiram Tindall, whom Bert now recognized as a farmer living just outside Lakeport. Occasionally he stopped with produce at the Bobbsey home. "What possessed you to do that, Nick?"

"A woman back there raised a window and called to me," stated Nick. "I had to see what she wanted. Maybe she wanted some berries."

"Well, good land o' Tunket!" snorted Mr. Tindall. "Couldn't you 'a' turned around and walked frontwards? Look at all them berries spoiled—wuth twenty cents a quart, too!"

"It was all his fault!" declared Nick again. "Why didn't he steer around me!"

"I tried to," retorted Bert. "But you kept on backing up, and you didn't even stop when I yelled to you."

"A crazy way to do!" declared Mr. Tindall. "Somebody's got to pay me for them berres!"

"I won't pay!" cried Nick.

"Then I'll take it out of your wages Saturday night!"

"If you do, I'll take it out of him—I'll fight him!" cried Nick, who was working himself up into a great rage. "I'll fix him!"

Quite a crowd had gathered by this time, the two men who had taken Bert's part still standing there, and one repeated:

"It wasn't the fault of this boy on the bicycle. He did all he could to avoid the collision."

"It was his fault!" asserted Nick.

And then a voice Bert well knew asked:

"What's the matter?"

There stood his mother. Mrs. Bobbsey had made her way through the crowd and now appeared beside her son, whose clothing was ruffled and dusty and whose wheel still lay where it had fallen in the street amid the scattered berries, the roller skates still fast to the handle bars.

"This boy backed up against my bicycle when I was riding along," Bert explained to his mother.

"He bumped into me!" snarled Nick Dodge, who worked as a hired boy for the farmer.

"All I know is that I lost ten quarts of blackberries, worth twenty cents a quart, and somebody's got to pay for 'em!" declared the angry peddler. "If I don't get it any other way I'll stop it out of his wages!" and he pointed to the scowling Nick.

"Was it your fault, Bert?" asked Mrs. Bobbsey.

"No, Mother, really it wasn't," he answered. "I did all I could to steer away from him."

"It was the young peddler's fault," asserted one of the two men who had interfered in time to keep Nick from attacking Bert. "We saw it all."

"I'm glad my son wasn't to blame," went on Mrs. Bobbsey. "At the same time——"

"Somebody's got to pay me for my berries!" declared Mr. Tindall, who had other farm produce on his wagon. "I don't care whose fault it was, somebody's got to pay me for them berries!"

"That is just what I was going to speak about," said Mrs. Bobbsey quietly.

"Yes, why don't you quit talking so much and see what the lady has to say?" asked one of the men sharply.

"Oh, well——" began Mr. Tindall, who did not seem to recognize in Mrs. Bobbsey an occasional customer.

"I shall be willing to pay for the spilled berries rather than have you think my son was at all to blame," said Bert's mother. "I believe him when he says it was not his fault, but, rather than have you take the sum out of this lad's wages," and she pointed to Nick, "I will pay you myself," and she took out her purse.

"That isn't fair, Mother!" declared Bert. "It was his own fault!"

"That's right!" declared one of the two men. "He brought it on himself."

"Besides," added the other, "he can pick up almost half the spilled berries. If they're washed they'll be as good as ever."

"Yes, I think they will," said Mrs. Bobbsey. "I will tell you what to do," she went on to Mr. Tindall. "Pick up the best of the berries and deliver them to my house. I will pay for the ten quarts you say were spilled, but my cook can get something out of them to make jam after they are washed. That will end the matter."

"Yes'm, I s'pose 'twill," agreed Mr. Tindall. "I don't want to be mean, but I have to get paid for my produce, an' if Nick makes trouble he's got to fix it up. I guess maybe it was his fault."

"It was not!" snapped the ragged lad.

"Don't let me hear any more talk out of you!" threatened the farmer. "Now you pick up as many of them berries as you can. Get some empty boxes from the wagon and then take 'em to this lady's house. Where do you live, ma'am?" he asked. "And do you really want to pay me for ten quarts, if, say, you can get only about six quarts of berries out of 'em for jam? Is that right?"

"That is right," replied Mrs. Bobbsey, with a smile, taking out her purse. "I would rather lose the price of four quarts of berries than see this boy suffer, even if it was his fault."

"It wasn't!" snarled Nick. "That fellow on a bicycle ran into me!"

"Didn't I tell you to stop talking?" cried Mr. Tindall, who appeared to have as short a temper as his helper. "Now dry up and pick up them berries and take 'em to this lady's house. I'll go along and peddle, and you can catch up to me!"

"All right!" growled Nick Dodge, as, brushing some of the street dust off his clothes, he prepared to save as many of the spilled berries as possible. "But I'll get square with you—see if I don't!" he muttered under his breath as he shot an angry look at Bert. "I'll fix you all right. I know where you live and I'll be on the watch! I'll fix you!"

Unconscious of the threats being muttered against him, Bert was standing his wheel up and looking at it to see that it had suffered no damage. Luckily, aside from a bent spoke, it was all right.

"Where are you going?" asked his mother as the peddler's wagon rumbled on and the crowd began to scatter, leaving Nick to pick up the berries.

"Over to John's to trade my old skates for one of his fish poles," Bert answered. "Say, Mother," he went on earnestly, "this wasn't my fault at all. He backed into me."

"I suppose he did, yes."

"Then you shouldn't pay for berries you don't get."

"I don't mind that, son," said Mrs. Bobbsey gently. "It is the best way out of the matter. I wouldn't want to see that poor boy made to pay."

"He was mean!" declared Bert, rubbing his arm where he had been pinched. "He wasn't fair!"

"Perhaps not. All the more reason why we should be a bit more than fair." Bert was very proud of his mother then. She seemed to know just what to do.

"Thank you, gentlemen, for taking my son's part," went on Mrs. Bobbsey to the two men who had witnessed the accident.

"It wasn't your son's fault in the least," they assured her.

Then they walked on, and Bert, saying he would soon be home, rode away while Mrs. Bobbsey went on about her own affairs.

But back in the street, scooping up spilled berries, was a scowling lad who, looking in the direction of Bert Bobbsey on his bicycle, muttered again and again:

"Just wait! I'll fix you for this!"

CHAPTER VI

OFF TO CHERRY CORNERS

"All aboard!" cried Flossie Bobbsey.

"No, Flossie! You shouldn't say that!" objected Freddie. "This isn't a boat! It's an automobile!"

Indeed it was the big family car the Bobbsey twins were getting into this lovely morning early in July, preparing to start for Cherry Corners.

"I know it isn't a boat," rejoined Flossie. "Guess I know a boat when I see one!"

"Then what'd you say 'all aboard' for?" demanded Freddie. "They only say 'all aboard' when it's a boat. Don't they, Bert?"

"I guess so," answered the older Bobbsey boy, who was busy helping Sam Johnson put valises and packages in the car.

"Well, anyhow," went on Flossie, who liked to have what she said listened to, "we're going away and it's like a trip on a boat and I'm going to say 'all aboard' as much as I like. That's what the train conductor says. Doesn't he, Nan?"

"Yes, indeed!" answered Flossie's sister, with a laugh. "But never mind that now. Get in. There are lots of last things to do, and we must hurry if we are going to Cherry Corners."

"I'll help!" offered Flossie eagerly, and she ran back to the porch and took hold of a bundle, one of several that Dinah had brought out of the house.

But Flossie was in such a hurry, or else the bundle was too heavy for her, that halfway between the front steps and the car she dropped what she was carrying.

"Careful!" called Mrs. Bobbsey.

"Lucky it was only a package of books!" said Mr. Bobbsey, with a laugh. "If it had been dishes, though! What about them, my fat little fairy?" and he caught up the books and Flossie in his arms.

"If it had been dishes," said the little girl,

kissing her father vigorously, "I wouldn't have dropped them!"

"I wouldn't want to trust you!" chuckled Bert.

It was two days after the elder Bobbsey boy had bumped into Nick Dodge, spilling the berries. During the time that had passed Mr. Bobbsey had put his business affairs into such shape that he could go away with his family for several weeks. In a way, this was a business trip, since, having acquired Red Gate Farm at Cherry Corners, the lumber merchant wanted to see if he could make any money by selling cherries and other produce, and perhaps sell the farm to somebody else.

"Not that we are going into the farm business," said Mr. Bobbsey to his wife; "but since we have a farm, we might as well make the best of it, and, at the same time, give the children a summer vacation."

The trunks had been shipped by express, and now the Bobbsey family was almost ready to go. Included in the family were Dinah and Snap, the dog. It had been decided to leave Sam Johnson at home to look after the house.

"And Snoop, too!" insisted Freddie, speaking of the big black cat. "You'll look after Snoop, too, won't you, Sam?"

"'Deed an' I will dat, li'l fireman!" chuckled the colored helper.

"Ef he don't—I'll hab sumpin to say to him when I comes home!" exclaimed Dinah, shaking a fat finger at her husband.

At first Mr. Bobbsey had rather objected to taking Snap along, but Bert and Nan had said a summer in the country on a farm would not be any fun without their dog, so it was decided to put Snap in a crate, strap it on the back of the auto, and take him along that way.

Freddie and Flossie at first almost cried because Snoop was not to be taken, but their mother said:

"Cats don't like to make new homes. They feel strange in new places, and Snoop might run away and try to come back here, and so get lost on the way. Better leave him with Sam."

"Won't Snap run away, too?" asked Freddie.

"No, my dear. Dogs will make themselves at home in a new place much more quickly than cats. Besides, Bert has Snap quite well trained."

"I only hope he is trained well enough to stay in the crate after I put him inside," murmured Bert, who was almost ready to put Snap in the slatted box in which he was to travel. This was to be done the last thing before leaving.

"Because I don't want him cooped up any longer than he has to be," said Bert.

The last valises and packages were now put in the big car. There were also some boxes containing a lunch which Dinah had insisted on packing. Mrs. Bobbsey had said they could stop at a restaurant on the way to Cherry Corners, or, for that matter, wait until they arrived at the farmhouse before eating after the morning meal.

But Dinah, shaking her head, remarked:

"No, ma'am! Scuse me, Mrs. Bobbsey, but we got to hab some lunch fo' de chilluns—specially Flossie an' Freddie. Dey might git hungry!"

So Dinah had her way, as she usually had.

"Well, are we almost ready?" asked Mr. Bobbsey, who had been looking the car over, to make sure there was air in the tires, that he had plenty of gasoline and oil, and that the radiator was filled with water, since there were some steep hills on the way and the day was a hot one.

"About ready, I think," said his wife.

Flossie and Freddie climbed in beside Dinah on the back seat. Mrs. Bobbsey and Nan were to sit on the two small extra seats, and Bert was to ride in front with his father. But as yet Bert was not in his place. He had yet to put Snap in the crate, nail on the last slats, and then he and his father would strap the box on the back of the car, where a place had been made for it.

"Will you ever forget the time Freddie let all the air out of one tire just when we were going to start?" asked Nan of her mother.

"Oh, yes!" laughed Mrs. Bobbsey. "That was two years ago. He wanted to blow up his toy balloon that had gone down."

It had really happened that way. Freddie and Flossie each had a toy rubber balloon, but, in some manner, Freddie's went flat. The automobile stood out in front of the house and Freddie knew there was air in the big fat tires. So what did he do but unscrew the cap, and then loosen the valve and hold the mouth of his toy balloon over the nipple!

The air rushed out so fast that it not only filled Freddie's balloon, but burst it, and then the auto tire went flat and Mr. Bobbsey had to pump it up, which took some time.

So the children's father saw to it, this time, that the tires were all right. Then, Sam having been given his last instructions, Mr. Bobbsey went to where Snap was tied near the front steps and said:

"We'll crate the dog now, Bert!"

Snap had been softly and mournfully howling from time to time, and barking and whining, fearing that he was to be left behind. But now, when he saw Bert and Mr. Bobbsey approaching him, he seemed to know he was going to be taken along.

However, he did not appear to like the looks of the crate, and he hung back and tried to pull away when it was brought up.

"We're not going to hurt you, old fellow!" exclaimed Bert, patting his pet. "It will be all right." So Snap allowed himself to be lifted in, though he whined as if he did not like it.

The slats that had been left off to admit the dog were now nailed on, and Bert was helping his father carry the crate to the rear of the auto when Nan leaned over the side of the car and whispered:

"Bert, there's that mean peddler boy going past!"

"What boy?" asked Freddie, catching the words.

"Hush, dear," said his mother in a low voice. "Nan means the boy Bert ran into on his bicycle."

Indeed, at that moment, Nick Dodge was walking past with some vegetables in a basket. He had come again with Mr. Tindall to sell things from the farm. The wagon and Mr. Tindall were, however, in a side street.

Nick did not look in the direction of the Bobbseys, though he must have seen them and have remembered the house where he had had to deliver the spilled berries. And Bert and his father were so busy, fastening the dog crate on the auto, that they paid no attention to the other lad.

"There!" said Mr. Bobbsey at last, "I guess you'll ride there in comfort, Snap!"

"We must stop now and then to give him a drink of water," said Bert, as he walked around to get in the front seat. "He'll want it, on account of this being a hot day."

"Yes," agreed Mr. Bobbsey, "we must water Snap."

Just as Bert was climbing up to take his place he saw Nick Dodge turn and start walking back down the street. The unpleasant chap looked straight at Bert, too.

"I wonder if he's coming here to pick a fight?" mused Bert. But he said nothing to the others about it, and his father and mother, with Nan, Flossie, Dinah, and Bert himself were so busy seeing that every last thing was in and waving good-bye to Sam that they paid no attention to Nick.

For a moment Bert thought that Nick really was coming up to the car, but he did not, stopping just back of it, however, to listen to a lady from a house near by who had called to ask the price of carrots.

Then Bert heard his father say:

"Well, here we go—off for Cherry Corners!"

The automobile started, and Bert had no further chance to see what became of Nick Dodge. He did not realize what a part this mischievous lad was to play in their summer outing.

The auto rolled along through the streets of Lakeport and had reached the outlying section, where there were not so many houses, when a man on a corner pointed toward the rear of the auto and shouted:

"Your dog's getting out!"

A moment later there was a howl and a bark from Snap, and as Mr. Bobbsey put on the brakes suddenly Bert thought:

"I guess that Nick Dodge loosened some of the slats so Snap could get out! I hope Snap doesn't run off or go all the way back home!"

CHAPTER VII

THE BUMPITY BUMP

FIRST out of the auto was Bert Bobbsey. He was out almost before the car had come to a stop.

"Be careful, son!" called his father.

"I don't want Snap to get away!" exclaimed Nan's brother, as he ran around to the rear of the machine.

Just as the man on the street had said, Snap was getting out of the crate. The dog wriggled out through a hole either made by himself, or, as Bert had mentioned, by the mean boy. Down to the street dropped Snap.

"Come back here!" cried Bert. "Don't run away, Snap!"

But Snap had no such idea. He was not going to desert his little friends, and he ran up to Bert, wagging his tail.

"What's the matter, Snap?" asked Freddie.

"He was lonesome in that crate," added Flossie. "Let's take him in here with us."

"We haven't room, dear," objected her mother.

"If I catch hold of that Nick Dodge!" muttered Bert, "I'll fix him for letting my dog out. If that man hadn't seen our dog getting loose," continued Bert, pointing to the man who had walked on, "Snap might have been lost."

"I don't believe that peddler boy had anything to do with Snap's getting out," said Mr. Bobbsey, who was looking at the opened crate. "You didn't drive these nails in the slats hard enough, Bert, and Snap easily pushed them loose. Here, old fellow!" he called to the dog. "You must get into your coop!"

Flossie and Freddie began to laugh and Flossie said:

"I guess Daddy thinks our dog is a chicken, telling him to get into his coop!"

"He's bigger than any rooster!" added Freddie.

Snap whined a little in protest as Bert and Mr. Bobbsey lifted him back up into the crate. Then, with a hammer from his tool kit, Mr. Bobbsey nailed the slats on firmly.

"You won't get out again, old fellow!" said Bert. "But we'll soon be at Cherry Corners. Then you can run around as much as you like."

"Maybe he's thirsty," suggested Mrs. Bobbsey.

"Oh, do give him a drink!" begged Nan. "You can fill his tin over at that hydrant, Bert." She pointed down the road where a street sprinkling cart had halted to fill the big tank with water.

"That's a good idea!" declared her brother.

There was a tin basin in Snap's crate, and Bert ran with this to where a little stream was leaking out around the hydrant hose. He asked the man if he might take some water.

"Need it for your automobile?" asked the street sprinkler.

"No, for my dog," answered the boy.

"Take as much as you like," said the man. "Dogs need a lot of water in hot weather.

If you want me to, I'll back my cart up there and give him a sprinkle."

"No, thank you," said Bert, with a laugh, as he thought how queer it would look to see Snap in his crate beneath the spouting end of the sprinkling cart. "I guess Snap wouldn't like it. He likes to swim, but I never gave him a shower bath."

"Try it, sometime," advised the sprinkling cart man, as Bert, with the tin of water, hurried back to Snap. The animal gratefully lapped it up and then composed himself for sleep.

"Well, I guess we can start off again now," said Mr. Bobbsey, as he made sure not only that the crate was well fastened on the auto, but that the slats were tightly nailed.

"You didn't see anything more of that boy, did you?" asked Mrs. Bobbsey, who had alighted from the car.

"No," answered Bert. "But he was looking at us when we passed. I thought maybe he had sneaked up and loosened the slats."

"He would need to have done it very quickly to let Snap out," remarked Mr.

Bobbsey. "I don't believe he did. What did you say his name was?"

"Nick Dodge," answered Bert.

Hearing this Freddie suddenly began laughing.

"What's the matter?" asked his mother. "Is Flossie tickling you?"

"Oh, no!" chuckled the small Bobbsey twin. "But I was just thinking that boy's name is Dodge, but he didn't dodge and get out of the way when Bert ran into him on the bicycle, did he? He didn't dodge a bit."

"I didn't run into him," insisted Bert as his father drove the auto along a quiet country road. "He backed up right into me. It was all his own fault, and I'll tell him so if I see him again."

For perhaps an hour the Bobbsey family rode along, with nothing particular happening except that every now and then Mrs. Bobbsey or Nan would call attention to some beautiful view. Bert was busy talking to his father about what they would do on Red Gate Farm, and learned that Mr. Bobbsey expected to hire the cherries picked so he could sell them.

"I'll help pick," offered Bert.

"Yes, I think you and Nan can do some of the work," said Mr. Bobbsey, and Bert was sure it would be great fun. His father said he would pay him and Nan the same price for picking cherries as he had to pay the other pickers—about two cents a quart.

Now and then Bert would have his father stop the car so he might look and see that Snap was all right. Each time the dog was found curled up contentedly. He seemed to know that it was best for him to keep quiet until he reached the end of his journey.

At one of these stops, which happened to be made in front of a farmhouse, Bert noticed that Snap was panting hard with his tongue hanging out of his mouth, which is the only way dogs have of cooling off.

"I think he needs more water," decided the boy. "And as there's a well here, it's a good place to get him some."

"I'd like a drink, too," signed Flossie.

"So would I!" echoed Freddie, who seldom let his twin sister get ahead of him.

"If they have some cool milk I think it would do the children good," suggested their mother. "Perhaps you will ask about it, Dick," she said to her husband.

"Surely," he said and, running the car off the main road to a shady place on the grass beneath a big oak tree, Mr. Bobbsey and Bert prepared to get out. A little boy, about Freddie's age, was in the front yard of the farmhouse, playing with a toy wagon.

"Do you have any milk for thirsty children in your house, little boy?" asked Mrs. Bobbsey.

"No, sir—I mean no, ma'am. We hasn't any milk in the house," he answered, smiling.

"Oh, haven't you? That's too bad. No use going in then, Dick, except to ask if we may have some water," said the children's mother.

But the little boy went on:

"We keep all our milk down cellar where it's cool."

"Oh, isn't he cute!" whispered Nan to her mother.

"A dear!" agreed Mrs. Bobbsey. "And he's smart, too! The idea of knowing why the milk is kept in the cellar."

Mr. Bobbsey glanced back at his car to

make sure that it was well out of the way of traffic, and then walked up toward the farmhouse. A pleasant-faced woman came to the door.

"Have you lost your way?" she asked, smiling.

"No," answered Mr. Bobbsey, whom Bert had followed. "But I wonder if we can buy some of the milk your little boy says you keep down in the cellar so it will be cool?"

"Oh, is Roscoe out there?" inquired his mother. "I told him not to go outside the gate."

"He didn't," Mr. Bobbsey said, with a laugh. "He is still inside. But about the milk, and some water for our dog, may we get some?"

"Why, yes, of course. We often sell milk to auto parties, and you can easily pump some water from the well."

"I'll get the water if you'll take Mother and the children out some milk," offered Bert, and this was soon being done.

Mr. Bobbsey found that Roscoe, which was the little boy's name, had spoken the truth when he said the milk was kept cool down in the cellar. It was a most refreshing drink, and Snap again lapped up some cool water with grateful waggings of his tail.

Flossie and Freddie stared at Roscoe, and he stared at them, and after Mrs. Bobbsey had admired the flowers around the old-fashioned house, it was time to travel on again.

"Take care the little fellow isn't under the car," said Mr. Bobbsey to Roscoe's mother.

"Oh, he has been taught to keep out of the way of autos," she answered.

Indeed it was easy to note that Roscoe was in no danger, for he was standing inside the gate, and with thanks for the refreshment, for which the woman charged only a small price, the Bobbsey family started off.

But the auto had not rolled more than a few feet out from the shady nook where Mr. Bobbsey had parked it than there sounded behind it a strange, rumbling, clattering sound.

"What's that?" cried the children's father, always on the alert when he heard a strange noise in or around the car.

"It's a bumpity bump!" exclaimed Flossie.

"That's what it is—a regular bumpity bump!" added Freddie, who began laughing when he had climbed up on the seat and was looking out of the rear window of the machine.

"What in the world is a bumpity bump?" asked Mr. Bobbsey, as he brought the auto to a stop, after the rumbling, rattling noise had kept up until he reached the road.

"It's my little wagon!" called Roscoe, with a laugh. "I tied it on your auto so it would have a ride!"

"Why, that's just what the little rascal has done!" gasped his mother, running out through the gate. "Roscoe, what possessed you to do such a thing?" she asked, as she began loosening the tangle of string that the little boy had used to fasten the tongue of his toy cart to the rear bumper of the car.

"I wanted my wagon to have a ride all by itself," was his reason.

"He must have crawled around through the bushes at the back of your car and fastened it on while I was giving you the milk," said Mrs. Norton, which was the woman's name. "Roscoe," she added, severely, as she wheeled his cart back to him, "I told you to keep away from autos! I shall have to punish you for this!"

"The auto wasn't going, Mother," he said, his laughter now turned to the edge of tears. "And I was behind it, not in befront of it," which he thought should make a difference.

"No matter, I told you to keep away from cars, either in front or back," said Mrs. Norton, "and I must punish you, Roscoe," and she carried him crying into the house, while Mr. Bobbsey, now that the "bumpity bump" was taken off his car, drove away. The little wagon had made a bumpity-bump sound as Flossie and Freddie said.

"Poor little fellow!" murmured Nan as Roscoe's cries floated down the road.

"It is better that he should suffer a little now, and be taught a lesson," said Mrs. Bobbsey, "than later on he should be hurt beneath a car. Children must be taught to be careful."

"But he was cute," said Nan, and they all agreed with her.

For half an hour more Mr. Bobbsey drove

along quiet, shady highways. At last he stopped at a gasoline filling station for a supply. He asked the man how much farther it was to Cherry Corners.

"Cherry Corners!" was the exclamation. "Why, brother, you're away off your road! You took the wrong turn, I guess. You're away off! You'll either have to go back to Snowdon Center or else keep on to Rockville. This road doesn't go to Cherry Corners."

"That's too bad!" said Mr. Bobbsey.

"Oh, Mother, are we lost?" whispered Flossie.

Freddie, seeing an anxious look on his father's face, murmured:

"What are we going to do? Can't we ever get to Cherry Corners?"

CHAPTER VIII

THE FIRE ALARM

THE man at the gasoline station began to laugh. Looking at the serious faces of Flossie and Freddie, he asked the two small Bobbsey twins:

"Do you like lollypops?"

It was such a strange question, coming, as it did, right after Daddy Bobbsey had found out that he was lost, that the little boy and girl did not know quite what to make of it.

"Do you," asked the gasoline man more slowly, "like lollypops?"

"Why—er—now—yes—I guess so," replied Freddie, for the man seemed to be looking particularly at him.

"When Mother lets us have them," added Flossie. "We can't take any just before our meals."

"Well, it's a little while yet until dinner time," went on the man, still laughing as he turned back to go into his shed. "And if your mother says it is all right, I should like to give each of you two little ones a lollypop. And the two older children, also, if they aren't above that kind of candy."

Nan and Bert looked at each other and laughed, while Bert said:

"All candy is good."

"Mother, may we have the lollypops?" asked Flossie in a whisper.

"I didn't know you sold candy here," said Mr. Bobbsey, while, it seemed, his wife was trying to make up her mind what to say in answer to her little daughter's question.

"Sell candy? Bless you, no!" chuckled the man. "I sell gas and oil and things for cars, but not candy."

"Then how——?" began Mr. Bobbsey, when the man, who had gone into his station, came out with a box of the candy lumps on sticks. Each lollypop was wrapped in a piece of waxed paper to keep it clean.

"This is how it happened," explained the

man. "A candy peddler came up here the other day. He ran out of gas and he hadn't sold enough stuff to take any money in yet, so he gave me a box of lollypops for enough gas to take him to town where he could make a sale.

"Well, not being in the candy business myself, I decided I would give the lollypops away, and that's what I've been doing. Help yourselves, children," he continued, putting the box in the car—"that is if your mother says it's all right."

"Oh, I guess so," slowly answered Mrs. Bobbsey with a smile. "It will be some time until we reach Cherry Corners, I fear."

"Oh, not so long—the roads are good," explained the gasoline man. And while Flossie and Freddie were trying to decide what flavor lollypops they wanted, he went on in a whisper:

"I saw that your two little children were a bit frightened at the idea of being lost," and he leaned close to Mr. Bobbsey and pointed back to Flossie and Freddie, who were thinking now of nothing but the candy. "I love children. I don't like them to be frightened, and so I thought about my box of lollypops."

"It was very kind of you," said Mrs. Bobbsey.

"Don't mention it!" exclaimed the man good-naturedly. "I'm glad I had the candy. You know how it is with kids—when they think they are lost or any one with them is, it sets them off."

"Yes," agreed Mr. Bobbsey. "And Freddie and Flossie have been lost often enough to know how it feels. But I don't see how I missed the road to Cherry Corners. I was there only last week."

"There's a detour in the road now that wasn't there last week," explained the gasoline man. "They're making some repairs. You had to turn off at Hanover Center, didn't you?"

"Yes," answered Mr. Bobbsey.

"Well, that's where you got wrong, I guess," went on the man. "The signs aren't very plain. But you can either go back, as I said, to Snowdon Center, or you can keep along this highway until you get to Rockville, and turn left there after leaving the village."

"Which will be the quicker way?" asked Mr. Bobbsey.

"I should say keep on to Rockville."

"Then we will," decided Mr. Bobbsey, and while he was getting some gas and oil and while Bert was giving Snap another drink, Flossie and Freddie had decided on what kind of lollypops they wanted and had quite forgotten about being lost. After all, getting lost in an auto isn't very serious, as Mrs. Bobbsey explained later to the small twins.

Bert and Nan, not being "above" lollypops, also took a candy each, and the Bobbseys were soon on their way again, the children refreshing themselves with the sweets while Mr. and Mrs. Bobbsey talked about various matters connected with Red Gate Farm at Cherry Corners.

Though the gasoline man had said it was only a short run to Rockville, out of which ran the road to the village whither the auto party were going, it took longer than Mr. Bobbsey had counted on, and when noon came they were still many miles from their destination.

"We had better stop in the next town, pick out a good restaurant, and have lunch," decided Mrs. Bobbsey.

"Is everything gone that Dinah packed up?" asked Mr. Bobbsey. "I don't mind stopping to eat," he said, "for it will probably be late afternoon before we arrive. But if the children have eaten all Dinah's lunch and the milk we got at the bumpity-bump farm-house, and now some lollypops, it seems to me——"

"Oh, Dad!" exclaimed Bert, begging his father's pardon for interrupting him, "Dinah didn't put up hardly any lunch. We thought we would be at Cherry Corners at noon, and there were only a few sandwiches and some cookies and——"

"It's all gone!" broke in Flossie. "And I'm hungry now."

"So am I!" joined in Freddie.

"Well you have good appetites, that's all I have to say!" chuckled their father. "So we will stop at a restaurant."

"Oh, goodie!" murmured Nan, for she loved to dine in public places.

"Will it be all right to leave Snap outside

in the crate?" asked Bert. "Somebody might take him."

"It won't be that Nick Dodge, anyhow," declared Nan. "He's far behind."

"We'll park the car in a place it can be watched," decided Mr. Bobbsey, and this was done, there being a good location in front of the restaurant which was on the main street of the next town through which they passed. A boy out on the sidewalk offered to "mind" the auto, as he called it.

"And don't let anybody bother my dog," added Bert.

"I won't," promised the lad, who seemed very much in earnest. "I like dogs. I'll stay right near yours and talk to him."

Snaps eemed to appreciate having company, and when the Bobbseys went in to lunch, Bert noticed that the "minder boy," as Flossie called him, was petting Snap and that the dog was wagging his tail in friendly fashion.

The only thing out of the ordinary that happened at the meal was that Freddie upset a glass of water in his lap, but when his mother chidingly murmured: "Oh, my dear!" he said easily:

"It doesn't matter! It's a hot day and the water makes my legs nice and cool! I like it!"

The waiter and several men eating near the Bobbsey table laughed at this answer.

"Your dog's all right," the "minder boy" announced, as Bert and the others came from the restaurant. "But I guess he'd like to get out of that cage."

"I guess he would," Bert agreed. "Well, he'll soon be out if we don't get lost again."

"Where you going?" the boy asked.

"To Cherry Corners."

"Oh, I know where that is! It's a swell place! Lots of cherries there. Some farmers bring 'em here to sell 'em!"

Bert and Nan were glad to hear that the place where they were going was all it pretended to be.

Once more the Bobbseys were on their way, and by the middle of the afternoon they were on the right road to Cherry Corners. Various signs told them this, and Mr. Bobbsey stopped once or twice to inquire of garage men to make sure.

"We won't get lost again!" he declared.

They passed through the last village they would meet before arriving at the place where the four farms met at the crossroads, and soon were on a lonely highway.

"Are you sure this is the right way?" asked Mrs. Bobbsey. "I don't want to be lost again."

"It's all right!" her husband said. "The last sign said ten miles to Cherry Corners. It's a bit lonesome, but we'll soon be off this road."

They were approaching a house—the only one within a mile or two, it seemed—when suddenly, just as they came in front of it, they heard a voice screaming:

"Fire! Fire! Help! Help! I'm burning up!"

"Oh, stop, Dick!" begged Mrs. Bobbsey. "There's been an accident up in that house!"

From the place, while Mr. Bobbsey jammed on the brakes, the voice cried again:

"Help, quick! I'm burning up!"

CHAPTER IX

CHERRIES EVERYWHERE

BERT BOBBSEY followed his father out of the auto, Mr. Bobbsey leaping over the side door without stopping to open it.

"Be careful!" warned Mrs. Bobbsey.

"Can't I go?" asked Nan.

"No, dear! Stay here with me and the others," said her mother. "If there is anything to do, Bert and your father will attend to it."

"The house is on fire!" declared Flossie.

"I don't see any smoke," observed Freddie, "and there's always smoke where there's a fire. Please, Mother," he went on, "couldn't I get out with my little engine?"

"Mercy, no!" exclaimed his mother. "Not for the world!"

"But it is queer there isn't any smoke!"

added Nan, who was looking closely at the house.

"Maybe it's all on fire inside," suggested Flossie, "and the smoke hasn't had time to get out yet."

"I hope no one is hurt," murmured Mrs. Bobbsey, anxiously watching her son and husband speeding up the front walk.

Freddie went on, in the tone of one who ought to know:

"Always where there is a fire there is smoke!"

Meanwhile the voice fiom the lonely house called again:

"Fire! Fire! I'm all burning up!"

By this time Mr. Bobbsey, followed by Bert, had entered the house. There was no one around it, neither man, woman, nor child, and the shouted alarm did not seem to be bringing help. But then there were no other houses near.

"Be careful, Dick!" Mrs. Bobbsey called to her husband, as she saw him go in. As he did not answer, and becoming alarmed about him, the children's mother said to Nan:

"You stay here with Flossie and Freddie!"

"Where are you going?" Nan wanted to know.

"To see that your father and Bert do not get into danger. Also to help, if I can."

Freddie was very anxious as he saw his mother getting out of the automobile.

"I'd like to put that fire out with my engine!" he said.

"Freddie Bobbsey!" exclaimed his mother, very earnestly, "if you put one foot outside of this car until I come back, you will never go to Cherry Corners!"

This threat was such a severe one that Freddie drew back—already he was halfway out of the machine—and he said:

"All right, Mother, I'll stay in. And I'll help take care of Flossie."

"Nan's going to take care of me," observed the little girl. "And, anyhow, I'm not going to get out. I want to see the cherries."

"So do I!" decided Freddie, and he did not again ask if he might put the fire out with his toy engine.

As Mrs. Bobbsey hurried toward the house, inside which her husband and Bert had disappeared, she looked in vain for any sign of smoke or fire.

Just then a woman came up a side path. She had been after berries, it was plain, for she had a pail full.

"Do you live here?" asked Mrs. Bobbsey.

"Yes," was the answer. "Why?"

"I'm afraid your house is on fire," went on the mother of the twins. "My husband and son have just gone inside to see what they can do. Some one called an alarm of fire and begged for help, saying they were burning up!"

To the surprise of Mrs. Bobbsey the woman with the pail filled with berries did not seem alarmed, nor even surprised. Instead she smiled.

"I guess you don't understand," went on the mother of the Bobbsey twins. "I said your house is on fire, though we can't see any smoke, and some one called for help."

"I expect that was Polly," said the woman, still smiling. And then the voice called again:

"Help! Help! I'm on fire! I'm burning!"

"There! Hear that!" cried Mrs. Bobbsey.

"Yes, that's Polly," said the woman, calmly setting down her pail of berries and taking off her sunbonnet.

"But, my dear woman!" exclaimed Mrs. Bobbsey. "Aren't you going to do anything? What room is this Polly in, so my husband can get her out. The fire must be all in one room."

"There isn't any fire," said the woman, and now she was laughing, while Nan and the two smaller twins in the car, who heard what was being said, wondered what it all meant.

"There isn't any fire," went on the woman. "It's just Polly's trick."

"A trick!" exclaimed Mrs. Bobbsey. "I should think you'd try to teach her not to play such tricks. Some day there may be a real fire, and when Polly cries for help no one will answer."

Just then her husband and Bert came out of the house. Bert was laughing and Mr. Bobbsey was smiling.

"I don't think this is a joke," said Mrs.

Bobbsey, and to the woman she went on: "Why don't you teach Polly not to play such tricks?"

"I have tried to teach her," was the answer, "but she doesn't seem to learn. I guess she's too old a parrot to be taught anything more."

"*Parrot?*" cried Mrs. Bobbsey in great surprise.

"Yes, parrot," answered the woman.

"Oh!" and the mother of the twins looked a bit puzzled. "I thought Polly was a little girl playing tricks."

"It's a big red and green parrot in a cage, Mother!" explained Bert. "You ought to hear how plain she talks—just like a real person."

"Yes, Polly has a very natural voice," said the woman who had been after berries. "She fools a great many people. She used to fool us at first, calling out about a fire and that she was burning up. But we don't pay any attention to her now. I'm sorry if she caused you any bother."

"Oh, it wasn't any bother," said Mr.

Bobbsey. "We just happened to be passing, and we heard what we thought was a woman calling out about a fire."

"So we ran in," continued Bert. "But we couldn't even see any smoke. Then I saw the parrot. Who taught her to call out like that?"

"She used to belong to a fireman in the city, who lived next door to his engine house," explained the woman of the lonely house. "I suppose some of the firemen taught her this trick. She has played it ever since my husband got her from the man who used to own the parrot. At first it caused a deal of bother, but all the folks around here are used to Polly now, and pay no attention to her. It is only strangers she fools."

"She must have known we were coming," said Mr. Bobbsey, with a chuckle. "Well, I'm glad there was no fire."

"So am I," said the berry woman. "A fire in the country, in a lonesome place like this, is dreadful. I think hearing Polly talk so much about fire has taught us to be careful."

By this time, Nan, seeing that there was

nothing to be feared and knowing her mother would think it all right, had allowed Flossie and Freddie to get out of the car to come and see what it was all about. Especially as now the parrot had changed her cry to a song and she was chanting away about stormy winds and sailing ships and breaking waves.

"I think a sailor must have owned her before she became a fire engine parrot," said the berry woman, and the visitors agreed with her.

The children were much amused by the big green and red bird, who seemed to know she was showing off before company and talked, as the woman said, "a blue streak," whatever that meant.

"But we must be getting on," said Mrs. Bobbsey at length. "We have been most of the day on this trip."

"Where are you going?" asked the berry woman.

"To Cherry Corners," she was told.

"Ah, yes, I know the place. It is very nice there. Well, I wish you good luck the rest of the way."

The auto was soon rolling along again,

while the parrot once more took up the refrain:

"Fire! Fire! I'm on fire! I'm burning up!"

"I wish I had a bird like that," sighed Freddie. "I could have a lot of fun with her and my toy engine."

"Well, I'm glad you haven't got her," said his mother, with a smile.

Everything seemed to be going along nicely when once more the trip was under way. The auto was gliding swiftly, and the road was a pleasant one, beneath big trees. They were getting into a neighborhood now where there were more houses, and Mrs. Bobbsey, with a sigh of relief, read a sign which said it was only two more miles to Cherry Corners.

"I'll be glad to get there," she remarked.

A little later they arrived at the outskirts of a pretty village, where a sign over the post-office informed them that they had arrived.

"But I don't see any cherries here," complained Flossie.

"Nor I," added Freddie, and the little twins were much disappointed.

"We aren't out at the farms yet," said their father. "They lie just beyond the village. We'll be there in about five minutes."

At the end of that time the auto made a turn in the road and there, before the eyes of the Bobbsey twins, lay the four farms at the crossroads—four big farms, on each one of which were a number of cherry trees, giving the village its name.

"Oh, there are cherries everywhere!" exclaimed Nan as she looked at the laden trees.

"But they are not quite ripe yet," said her mother.

"No," answered Mr. Bobbsey. "Except for some early ones. The main crop of cherries will not be ripe for another week or two. But that time will soon pass."

"Which is Red Gate Farm?" asked Bert. But he saw for himself a moment later as his father guided the auto toward a big red gate behind which was a large, rambling, old-fashioned farmhouse. Red Gate Farm was on one corner of the crossroads, and on the other three corners were three more farms, though Red Gate was the largest.

"Well, you got here, I see," remarked an old man shuffling down the front walk. "A little late, aren't you?"

"Just a little," admitted Mr. Bobbsey. "We missed our road and we had an adventure on the way. Is everything all right?"

"Oh, yes. I got all the groceries in you told me about, and I would have had my wife cook something, only you said you were going to bring a cook."

"Yes, we have her with us," and Mr. Bobbsey motioned to Dinah, who had been sleeping half the time on the trip. She used to say:

"Auto ridin' done make me pow'ful drowsy!"

"Who is that old gentleman, Mother?" asked Nan.

"He is a sort of caretaker your father hired after he took over Red Gate Farm," Mrs. Bobbsey explained. "He has been here looking after things until we could arrive. I forget his name."

But the children heard it a minute later when their father said:

"All right, Mr. Tason, and thank you for looking after things. I imagine we shall soon begin picking cherries, sha'n't we?"

"In another week. Have you any pickers engaged?"

"Not yet. How do I get them?" asked Mr. Bobbsey, as Bert and Nan were helping Dinah and their mother take the things out of the car.

"Oh, there'll be plenty of men, women, and boys coming to you for the work soon," said Mr. Tason. "Or if you like, you can have Mr. Tansy get you some pickers."

"Who is Mr. Tansy?" asked Mr. Bobbsey, while the children were looking around at the many trees, all laden with half-ripe cherries.

"He's the man who runs Oak Tree Farm," and Mr. Tason pointed to one diagonally across the way from Red Gate. "There he is now," he added, and he called to a farmer who was coming out of his gate:

"Hi, Sam, got any extra cherry pickers you can let Mr. Bobbsey have?"

"Why, yes, I reckon so," was the drawling answer. "I've hired about all I need. I got a letter from one feller to-day who says he's pretty good at picking. Let's see—where did I put that note? Oh, here it is," and Mr. Tansy took a paper from his pocket. "His name's Nick Dodge and he writes me he's tired of working for a peddling truck farmer and wants to get out on a big place. But I hired all I needed before I got his note. You might want to hire this Nick Dodge, Mr. Bobbsey," and he walked over toward Red Gate Farm.

Bert and Nan looked at each other. It seemed a strange thing to hear the name Nick Dodge again.

"I don't believe it's the same one," whispered Nan to her brother.

"I don't know," mused Bert. "It seems as if it might be when he speaks of working for a peddling truck farmer. But I guess he won't get any work on Red Gate if it is the same fellow!"

CHAPTER X

NICK IN A TREE

MR. BOBBSEY, also, seemed much interested in hearing the name of Nick Dodge, for he remembered what his wife and Bert had told about the unpleasant peddler boy who had tried to make trouble for Bert.

"How did you hear about this Dodge lad, Mr. Tansy?" asked Mr. Bobbsey.

"Oh, there's an employment agency in Lakeport—that's where you live, I hear. There's an agency there where we farmers write to get help. Men and boys who want to go about the country picking cherries, helping get in hay, and the like of that, send their names to the office or else they go there, find out what farmers need help, and then write for jobs.

"I got a lot of letters from men and boys who wanted to pick my cherries, and there was one from this Nick Dodge. But, as I say, I have all the pickers I need, so you can have this Nick if you want him."

"Better think about it," said Mrs. Bobbsey in a low voice to her husband as she heard this talk. "It might not be the same boy who made trouble for Bert, but, again, it might be. I'd wait, and find out for sure."

"I will," answered the children's father, and he said to Mr. Tansy: "Thanks, but I'll wait a while. My cherries don't ripen as soon as yours, so I will have time enough."

"Yes," agreed the other farmer, "you will. And when it comes time for your cherries to be picked you'll be swamped by a crowd of pickers from around here. You won't have any trouble, even if you don't hire this Nick Dodge. I'll just write back and say I don't need him."

By this time Mrs. Bobbsey, with the help of Nan, Bert, and Dinah, had about emptied the auto of the baggage and other things brought to Red Gate Farm. Of course the first thing Bert did was to get his dog out of the crate and tie Snap securely to a post in the shade, with plenty of cool water.

Flossie and Freddie played about near their pet, talking to him, and very likely Snap soon felt quite at home. After all, it did not much matter to him where he was as long as the children were around him.

Mr. Bobbsey remained a little longer talking to Mr. Tansy and finding out about the other two farms at Cherry Corners. You remember there were four, which, meeting at a place where two roads crossed, made the corners. Mr. Bobbsey owned one of the farms—Red Gate, and diagonally across from him, or "kitty-corner," as Flossie called it, was Mr. Tansy's place. The other farms were owned by a Mr. Winton and a Mr. Searl.

"Well, how is everything?" asked Mr. Bobbsey of his wife and the children as he walked over near where the now empty car was parked.

"All right," answered Mrs. Bobbsey. "Dinah is inside getting supper."

"It's lovely here," said Nan. "We can have lots of fun."

"Where is the place where I can go fishing?" asked Bert, who had brought along a rod and quite a collection of hooks and lines.

"I don't just know," his father answered. "This place is a bit strange to me. I haven't owned it long. Perhaps Mr. Tason can tell you," and he looked at the elderly man who had been engaged as a caretaker.

"There's a little river about half a mile down the road," was the answer. "I'll show you to-morrow."

"And where are all the cows and chickens and horses and sheep and things like that?" asked Flossie, who loved animals.

"There isn't much stock on Red Gate," her father told her. "When I took over the farm I knew I wouldn't have time to bother with horses and cows, so I let them be sold. But we have some chickens, I believe?" and he looked a question at Mr. Tason.

"Yes, there's quite a flock of hens," was the answer. "But if the children like cows and horses and such animals, they'll find plenty on the other three farms," and this turned out to be true.

"If there are any fires that need putting out, I'll do it," Freddie Bobbsey called to Mr. Tason, as the latter was leaving, having now turned the farm and house over to Mr. Bobbsey.

"Oh, you put out fires, do you?" asked the caretaker, with a laugh.

"I have my engine!" went on the little fellow, and proudly he showed his toy, having already filled the tank with water from the kitchen sink and wound up the spring that worked the pump. "Look at it squirt!" cried Freddie.

"That's a noble engine!" declared Mr. Tason. "If I see any fires I'll let you know," and the little chap was quite pleased at hearing this.

The quaint, old-fashioned home that went with Red Gate Farm was furnished with everything needed to keep house, and Dinah, though she said the kitchen was not nearly so good as the one at home, admitted that it would do very well.

"I'll soon hab sumpin to eat fo' mah honey lambs," she said, meaning the children.

"They can't be very hungry," remarked their mother. "It seems to me they did nothing but eat all the way here, and we were a long while on the road."

"I'm hungry!" admitted Bert, and as the others said the same thing, Dinah knew she need not fear any of her food going to waste. It did not take long to get settled in the old house, and after supper the family roamed about the place, noting how many cherry trees there were. The children were eager to pick some to eat, but Mr. Bobbsey would not allow this, as there were only one or two trees where the fruit was just beginning to turn red.

"We'll have plenty of cherries a little later," he said, "and if we need any to eat before then, we can get some from either of the other three farms."

"I'd like to get some for a cherry pie," said Mrs. Bobbsey.

"Oh, could I make a pie?" begged Nan, and her mother said she might.

"Can I feed the chickens?" begged Flossie. Freddie, hearing this, also pleaded to be allowed to help.

"That's so—the chickens!" exclaimed Mr. Bobbsey. "I almost forgot about them. They ought to have been fed before this."

But when the whole family went out to the

henhouse they found the fowls had gone to roost, and, looking in the door, the children saw the feathered creatures huddled on the roost, some with heads under their wings.

"I hope they didn't go to bed hungry," said Mr. Bobbsey.

Just then a young man, who seemed to be a hired man on one of the adjoining farms, passed down the road near the henhouses and, seeing the Bobbsey family, he called:

"Are you wondering about your hens?"

"Yes," replied the children's father, "I was saying I hoped they had been fed."

"They were," said the hired man. "I saw Mr. Tason scattering grain to them just before you arrived."

"Oh, thank you! Then they're all right," Mr. Bobbsey remarked, and to the children he said, looking at Bert particularly: "I shall give you four charge of the chickens, you must feed them and gather the eggs."

"That will be fun!" exclaimed Nan.

"I'm going to gather eggs!" declared Flossie.

"Well, don't fall in them the way you did once!" begged Bert, with a laugh, remembering something that had happened at Meadow Brook.

There was too much to see at Red Gate to permit of its all being viewed in one evening, and when it grew dark Mrs. Bobbsey insisted that Freddie and Flossie should go to bed, as they were tired with the day's travel. Nan and Bert were allowed to remain up a little longer, but soon the old farmhouse was quiet and all were asleep save Snap, who roved about, making sure that those he guarded would come to no harm in the night.

By daylight the farm looked even more pleasing than it had in the evening, and Mrs. Bobbsey was sure it would prove a wonderful place to spend the summer. Mr. Bobbsey went off after breakfast to inquire about selling his cherries when they should ripen, for the crop would have to be sent to a distant city to be disposed of.

In spite of what their father had said about there being as yet no ripe cherries at Red Gate, the Bobbsey twins, hoping against hope, visited tree after tree. Though nearly every one was laden, still none was fit to be picked.

However, Mrs. Bobbsey, who received an

early call from Mrs. Tansy, solved the problem, for she said:

"Children, Mr. Tansy has a tree of early cherries and he will let you have some to eat."

"Oh, hurray!" cried Bert.

"Could I make a pie?" asked Nan.

"You may have all the cherries you need for pies," said Mrs. Tansy, with a laugh.

A little later, when the children had eaten as much of the delicious fruit as was good for them, Nan made her pie. She really did very well, for her mother and Dinah had taught her something about kitchen work, and though the fat black cook kept a watchful eye over the baking of the pastry, Nan really did most of the work herself.

"And it's a lovely pie!" exclaimed her father, as he ate some at supper that night. Nan blushed with pleasure.

All that day the Bobbsey twins had played around Cherry Corners, and Bert went fishing, but caught nothing. However, this did not discourage him.

"You sort of have to get acquainted with the fish in a new place," he said.

When night came the children were ready

for bed, but they were up bright and early the next morning.

However, if the children were bright, the weather was just the opposite, for it rained. But there was a big attic in the farmhouse, and going up there the twins found plenty with which to amuse themselves. There were some bound magazines, some story books, some strings of sleigh-bells from the days of old, before automobiles were invented, and a lot of old soldier clothes that, so Mr. Bobbsey said, had belonged to the son of the man from whom he had bought the place.

So the rainy day passed pleasantly in the attic, and the sun came out the next day, which made everything all right. Even though it had rained, the children kept to their task of feeding the chickens, and Flossie and Freddie were delighted when they were allowed to carry in about a dozen eggs, which Dinah put carefully away.

Two or three more days passed, and on each one the warm sun brought nearer to ripeness the cherries on the trees at Red Gate. But it would yet be a full week before any were ready to pick. However, some of the early fruit on the other farms was being gathered and several men and boys had been hired as pickers. Seeing them busy in the trees, Bert said to his father:

"Do you think, Daddy, I could hire out to Mr. Tansy, or one of the other cherry farms, and pick cherries until ours are ripe?"

"Well, I hardly think it would be worth while," was the answer. "You couldn't pick fast enough to make it an object for any of the other farmers to hire you, and you will soon be busy here. But, if you like, you may go over to some of the other places and watch in order to learn how cherries are picked."

"That'll be fun!" decided Bert. "Come on, Nan! You'll want to learn, too! We'll both pick when our cherries are ripe."

Flossie and Freddie had gone on a little picnic with their mother, which left Nan and Bert free to go where they pleased. So they strolled across the road and down a lane that led to the farm and cherry orchard of Mr. Winton. He had the most early cherries of any of the four corner properties.

Up in the trees or standing on ladders

thrust up into them were a number of men and boys. As Bert and Nan passed under one tree, meanwhile looking about and seeing how the fruit was gathered and put into baskets, Bert heard an exclamation.

It came from a tree under which he and his sister were standing, an exclamation as of surprise. And Bert, looking up, was himself surprised, for he saw in the tree Nick Dodge, who was filling a pail with red cherries.

"There he is, Nan!" said Bert in a low voice.

"Who?"

"Nick Dodge! The boy who was going to fight me because he backed into my bicycle! He's up here—at Cherry Corners!"

From his tree Nick looked down at Bert Bobbsey.

CHAPTER XI

BERT'S MUD BATH

WHETHER Nick Dodge would have said anything to Bert and his sister or whether the quarrelsome chap might have thrown some soft cherries at the elder Bobbsey twins never was found out, because just at that moment Mr. Winton, the owner of the farm, came walking through the orchard to see how his cherry pickers were working. He caught sight of Bert and Nan, and knew who they were.

"Looking for jobs?" the orchard owner asked pleasantly.

"No, thank you," Bert answered. "My father said we should come over to see how the cherries were picked so we'd know how to do it when ours got ripe."

"A good idea!" declared Mr. Winton.

"Make yourselves at home and eat as many as you like."

"I should think," said Nan, with a smile, "that if you told every one that, you wouldn't have many cherries left to sell."

"Oh, shucks," chuckled Mr. Winton, "I've got loads of cherries! Your father will have also, only his will be later than mine. What few you two will eat won't be a drop in the bucket—no more than what the robins and catbirds take. I always tell my pickers when I hire them," he went on, "to eat all the cherries they can hold. They most always do—the first day," and he laughed again. "But after that they get tired of them and they pick instead of eating. It's just like working in a candy shop—the first week you may eat a lot, but after that—no more!"

He looked up into the tree where Nick was perched and, observing the new hand, asked: "How you making out, bub?"

"Oh, all right!" answered Nick

"You'll have to pick a bit faster than that, though, if you expect to make more than your board and lodging," went on the farmer. "Be lively."

"All right," half growled Nick, and he did not again look down at Bert and Nan.

"You see we hire cherry pickers and pay them so much a quart, and board and lodge them besides," said Mr. Winton. "If a man or a boy picks only enough to cover what he eats and the cost of his lodging, he isn't going to make money and we don't like laggers. They must make their fingers fly if they expect to take away any money when the season ends. And between you two and me," went on the farmer in a whisper as they moved away from the tree where Nick was, "that fellow isn't all he cracked himself up to be."

"Did he say he was a good picker?" asked Bert.

"He did in the letter he sent me asking for work," replied Mr. Winton. "You see he got my name from the employment agency in Lakeport, and he wrote that he was a fast picker. But I don't think much of him! He's too slow! I don't like him!"

"I don't either," said Bert.

"Do you know him?" asked Mr. Winton quickly. "Was he bothering you? I mean throwing cherries at you? Some of the boy pickers are a bit mischievous. If he bothered you——"

"He didn't now," explained Bert. "But I had a run-in with him back in Lakeport before we came here."

"Oh, that's so—you're from Lakeport, aren't you? But what about this lad?" and he looked back toward the tree in which Nick could be seen moving from limb to limb.

"Oh, it wasn't anything very much," Bert answered, and he told the story of the quarrel with Nick Dodge. "It was his own fault that he tumbled and spilled the berries," added Nan's brother.

"Seems like it was," commented Mr. Winton. "There's a funny thing about this Nick—I must tell you," and he chuckled. "You see, when we hire pickers by letter we don't know them and they don't know us, except by name. Well, I was standing at my front gate the other evening when some of my pickers came up from the city. This Dodge fellow was one of the last. He must have got his directions wrong, for I saw him start to go into your place, thinking it was mine."

"Did he?" asked Bert. "I didn't notice."

"You and your mother were on the front porch at the time," went on Mr. Winton, "and when this fellow saw you, though you may not have seen him, he turned away, and later one of my hired men heard him say he'd never work there."

"No, I guess my father wouldn't have him!" remarked Nan, with a little uptilting of her nose. "Especially after the mean way he acted toward my brother."

"No, I guess you wouldn't want him on your cherry farm—it wouldn't be exactly pleasant," agreed Mr. Winton. "But I had no quarrel with him, and I didn't know this at the time. Anyhow, he mistook your place for mine, and I guess after he saw you and your mother, Bert, and remembered what had happened, he was going to give up the job.

"But he found out he was in the wrong stall, so he switched over here, and, as he said he was a good picker, I hired him. But he's got to work faster than he is doing, or I won't keep him," concluded the farmer.

"Now walk around as much as you like, help yourselves to cherries off the trees, and see how the work is done," invited Mr. Bobbsey's neighbor.

Bert and Nan took advantage of Mr. Winton's kindness, though, remembering their mother's warning, they did not eat much of the fruit. But they saw how the cherries were picked first into large pails or baskets by men and boys who climbed up into trees or stood on ladders that extended up amid the laden branches. When the pails and baskets were filled the pickers carried them to a shed where each was given a slip to show how much he had picked. At the end of the week the pickers were paid according to these slips, their board and lodging being deducted.

In the shed the cherries were sorted over, packed into boxes or quart strawberry baskets and put into crates which were shipped to distant cities.

The cherry picking season does not last very long, and the work must be done fast, for the fruit ripens quickly after it gets past the green stage. The pickers do not make fortunes, but the work is pleasant and after the cherries are gathered there are other crops they can help harvest, so they drift about from farm to farm, making enough to live on in the summer at least.

Nan and Bert observed how the work was done, and were eager for the time to come when they might gather the cherries on Red Gate Farm. On their way home the brother and sister talked of having seen Nick.

"Shall you tell Mother he is up here?" asked Nan.

"Oh, yes," decided Bert. "It will be best. He may not make any more trouble, but it's best to tell."

"I think so, too," agreed Nan.

Mr. and Mrs. Bobbsey were not surprised, neither were they alarmed on hearing that Nick Dodge had left the neighborhood of Lakeport and was in Cherry Corners.

"He is a sort of rover, I guess," commented Mr. Bobbsey. "I don't want him on my place, and I guess, according to what Mr. Winton said, he will not come here. If he makes any trouble for you, Bert, let me know."

"Try not to have anything to do with him," suggested Mrs. Bobbsey. "He is an unreasonable boy, I'm afraid. I do hope there won't be any fighting!"

"I'm not going to run away from him!" declared Bert.

"No, I wouldn't want you to do that," said his father. "But don't be the one to start a quarrel," and Bert promised he would not.

The next day Bert decided to go fishing again, hoping for better luck. He asked Nan to go with him, but she said she was going to bake a cake, and promised Bert a piece when he returned from his trip.

"That'll be fine!" he exclaimed. "I'm always hungry when I come back from fishing!"

Freddie teased to accompany his brother, but as Bert was really anxious to have some luck this time, and knew Freddie would be so restless as to prevent his remaining long in one spot, he promised to take the little fellow some other day.

Sitting on the shady bank of the stream where there was an eddy, or deep, slow current, Bert baited his hook and cast in. Hardly had the cork float ceased bobbing on the surface than it was suddenly pulled under.

"I got a bite!" Bert excitedly whispered to himself, and he had. It was more than a bite, for it was a good-sized fish which the boy soon landed on the grassy bank.

"This is my lucky day!" Bert told himself with shining eyes, and so it proved, for, though his largest fish got off the hook and dropped back with a great splash, still Bert managed to pull in enough for what Dinah said was "suah de bes' mess ob fish ever I done see!"

With his string of prizes dangling at his side, Bert started home in the early evening. As he was walking along the edge of the brook, in a dark, shadowy place, Bert suddenly heard the crackling of broken sticks, which told of some one walking not far away from him.

"Wonder who it is," thought the Bobbsey lad. "Hope it isn't Freddie. If he followed me the folks will think he is lost." But he did not hear his small brother calling, as Freddie would have done.

Bert looked down at his fish, proud of his luck and success, and he was wondering what his father and mother would say, when suddenly there was a rustling in the leaves, and through the bushes came a big ball of soft, sticky mud. It struck Bert on the back of his neck, splashed up into his face and over his clothes, and spattered him generally, giving him a most unpleasant shower bath.

CHAPTER XII

UPSIDE DOWN

"HEY there! Who's doing that? What do you mean—splashing mud on me?" cried Bert.

He dropped his string of fish and pulled out his handkerchief as he stood there in the woods, wondering who had played this mean trick on him—for it was a mean trick. Some of the mud and water with which it was mixed had splattered around to Bert's face—some was running down the back of his neck, inside his shirt, and there was a good deal on his clothes. Luckily it was an old suit—his mother insisted on Bert's wearing old clothes when he went fishing.

"Who did that?" cried the boy again, as he prepared to wipe his face on his handkerchief. No one answered, but Bert heard the crackling of broken branches and knew some one was running away. He also heard a mocking laugh.

Wiping muddy faces on handkerchiefs is not so good for the handkerchiefs. But Bert had already dirtied his by wiping his hands on it after taking several fish off his hook, and he reasoned that the square of cambric would not suffer much more if he cleaned his face with it. This he did, wiping off as much as possible of the mud and water.

Then the boy looked about him, trying to discover who it was that had thrown the mud ball. The ball was of soft, mushy mud —freshly made.

"It was some fellow who threw that, and I can pretty nearly guess who it was," murmured Bert, as, having cleansed himself as best he could, he picked up his string of fish and started homeward again. "It was that Nick Dodge!"

If Bert could have met the cherry-picking lad then I think there would have been a fight. Bert was very angry, and rightly so. But though he peered this way and that through the bushes and amid the trees, he caught no glimpse of Nick. That youth, if, indeed, it was he who had showered Bert with mud, had made his escape.

"He must have sneaked up when I was fishing," decided the Bobbsey boy, "and then he waited until he saw me coming along and he plastered me! He plastered me good!"

Part of the lump of mud, after striking Bert in the back of the neck, had fallen on the path in a mass, water oozing from it. Bert saw that it was the kind of mud that was plentiful on the bank of the stream where he had been fishing.

"All right, Nick Dodge!" murmured Bert as he wended his way homeward. "I'll get square with you for this. Just you wait!"

Flossie and Freddie saw Bert coming up the back garden path with his string of fish, and Freddie cried:

"Oh, look what a lot Bert caught!"

"He fell into the water, too," added Flossie when she saw her brother's muddy condition.

"What's that? Did you fall in, Bert?" asked his mother, who heard, from where she was sitting on the side porch, what the small twins said.

"No, I didn't fall in, Mother."

"But you are all wet and muddy!" declared Nan, who, having finished making her cake, was sitting with her mother.

"Somebody plunked me with a mud ball," explained Bert with a rueful smile. "And I think it was that Nick Dodge," he added, as his father came out of the house. Then Bert explained what had happened and Mr. Bobbsey said:

"Keep cool, Bert. You aren't sure it was Nick, and if you accuse him just because you guess so, it will only lead to more trouble. But I will speak to Mr. Winton and have him keep a little watch over this lad. If he does such tricks as that he isn't the kind we want at Cherry Corners."

"Oh, I won't say anything to him," promised Bert. "But if I catch him throwing any more mud at me——"

"You mustn't fight!" quickly interposed Mrs. Bobbsey.

"But you don't want me to stand still and let him cover me with more mud, do you, Mother?"

"No, not exactly——Oh, dear! Why did

that unpleasant boy have to come up here and spoil our nice vacation?" sighed Mrs. Bobbsey.

"I don't believe he'll do it again," decided her husband. "I will take a hand in affairs if he does."

So the matter was allowed to rest for a time. There was no real proof that Nick had thrown the mud, and it might well have been some other lad, who had no intention of hitting Bert. But all signs pointed to young Dodge.

Bert gave his fish to Dinah, who soon cleaned them to fry for supper, and Bert went up to the bathroom to wash himself, for there was running water, as well as other city improvements, in the farmhouse.

Nan's cake was a great success, and she was proudly allowed to cut it herself and pass it around.

"What you giving Bert such a big piece for?" asked Freddie, as he noticed his brother's helping.

"Because he brought home fish for us to eat," explained Nan. "And he got hit with a mud ball," she added.

"I'll let Flossie hit me with a mud ball if you'll give me a big piece of cake," offered Freddie eagerly, but his mother, with a laugh, warned the two smaller twins against any such trick as that.

Two or three days more passed happily for the Bobbsey twins at Red Gate Farm at Cherry Corners. They wandered over the meadows and went on excursions to the woods, either by themselves or with their father and mother. And Snap, the faithful dog, always went with them. He had forgotten all about the sad time he had had shut up in a crate on the back of the auto, and was happy now.

Mr. Bobbsey was taking a well-earned vacation from his lumber business, planning to remain at Red Gate until after his cherries were picked.

"And we'll start in about four days more," the children's father decided.

There were murmurs of delight from the four children at this, and they thought the days would never pass quickly enough. Several times, morning and afternoon, they would go out to look up into the trees, to see how the cherries were ripening.

In order that they should not be crushed to pulp on their journey to the city in crates and baskets, the cherries were picked a little while before they were "dead ripe."

The day before the picking was to begin, Bert went fishing again, this time taking his small brother with him.

"And if anybody throws mud at you I'll catch 'em on my fishhook!" declared Freddie.

However, nothing like this happened, though more than once, when Bert was quietly fishing and Freddie was doing his best to be patient and wait for a bite, the little fellow would exclaim:

"I think I hear somebody coming, Bert! Maybe it's Nick going to sling more mud!"

But the unpleasant lad was not seen. Indeed, he was busy picking cherries on Mr. Winton's farm. So Bert and Freddie fished in peace and brought home another "mess" for Dinah to cook.

Then, the next day, cherry picking started at Red Gate.

Ladders were placed up in the taller trees, stepladders were put beneath smaller trees and, climbing up, the pickers began to gather the lovely red and black fruit, while other men helped Mr. Bobbsey sort and pack it in the little shed erected for this work.

Nan and Bert were allowed to pick with the regular workers, and Mr. Bobbsey said he would pay his two older children just as much as he paid the pickers he hired. Nan got up on a stepladder, but Bert chose to go up a taller ladder into one of the higher trees.

Of course, Flossie and Freddie teased to be allowed to pick, and they were so anxious to "help," as they called it, that their mother found a low tree from which, by standing on upturned boxes, the small twins could gather fruit.

"But you mustn't climb up into the tree," warned Mrs. Bobbsey.

However, Freddie did not obey. Having reached all the cherries he could, by standing on the box, he decided he would get up into the tree. So, saying nothing to Flossie, who was on a box opposite him, Freddie scrambled up.

But something went wrong. Either his feet or his hands slipped, and a moment later Flossie, who was surprised at her brother's action, was more startled when he cried:

"Oh! Oh! I'm upside down!"

That is exactly what Freddie was. He had fallen out of the low tree. Had he slipped all the way he would not have been hurt, for the grass was thick beneath it. But he slipped only part of the way out, and then his right foot, catching in a crotch, or Y-shaped branch, held the little boy there, with his feet in the air and his head toward the ground, and only a short distance from it.

"I'm upside down!" wailed poor Freddie.

CHAPTER XIII

THE CIRCUS TRAIN

BERT BOBBSEY, who was at the upper end of the ladder he was using to pick cherries, heard his small brother's call for help. He turned at once to see what the trouble was.

As soon as Bert caught sight of Freddie hanging upside down by one foot, he started down in a hurry, having fastened his pail, half filled with cherries, to a rung of the ladder by means of a wire hook in the shape of the letter S.

"I'll get you, Freddie!" called Bert.

But Nan, who was nearer her little brother and not so far up on her ladder, was the first to reach Freddie. She murmured words of sympathy, and told Flossie, who was also crying, to keep quiet.

"Freddie isn't hurt!" said Nan.

"But he's standing on his head!" sobbed Flossie.

"Well, I'll soon have him on his feet," answered Nan. And she did.

She took hold of Freddie by his shoulders and lifted him. This took the weight off the leg that was caught in the crotch of the tree and Freddie found that, by kicking a bit, he could free himself. This he did, and a moment later he was standing upright beside his two sisters, for Flossie, after seeing her brother's plight, had gotten down off her perch.

"Now don't do that again!" warned Nan, when she saw that the small boy was all right. "Mother told you to keep out of the tree!"

"But I just wanted to reach some big, red cherries," gasped Freddie, for his breath was coming in spasms after his frightened crying spell.

"No matter!" added Bert, who by this time was off his high ladder. "You must keep out of trees, or else Mother won't let you pick any more cherries."

"All right—I will!" Freddie promised. "I'll stay on the box."

"I got a lot more cherries picked than Freddie did," observed Flossie, showing her pail, the bottom of which was covered two or three inches deep with the round, red fruit.

"Well, I spilled mine, or I'd have a lot more than you!" said Freddie. This was true enough. For when he slipped from the tree his pail turned upside down, just as Freddie himself had done, and now the cherries were scattered on the ground.

"Oh, dear!" sighed Freddie, when he saw what had happened.

"Never mind. I'll help you pick them up," offered Nan kindly. Though Flossie had boasted over her success, she, too, joined with Nan in gathering from the ground all the cherries fit to be saved, so that soon Freddie's pail again had red fruit in it.

Bert, after making sure that his brother was all right, went back to his ladder, for the older Bobbsey lad was very much in earnest about this cherry picking—more earnest even than Nan.

"I want to earn some money to buy a new

fish pole," Bert had said to his mother. "I'd get a lot more fish if I had a new pole."

"I don't believe fish are particular what kind of a pole they are caught on," Mrs. Bobbsey had answered, with a smile.

"It isn't the pole so much as it is the reel," Bert said. "If you can't reel in your line quickly after you get a bite, the fish gets off the hook. I want a new pole and reel." This was why he was so much in earnest in picking cherries. Nan had no special object in earning money at this time, though she said she might earn enough to buy a new book or two.

The excitement caused by Freddie's tumble was soon over, and some of the men and boys who had been hired for the work and who had gathered at the tree to help the little fellow, went back to their tasks, as Bert had done.

Mr. Bobbsey, at the other end of the orchard, heard of what had happened, and, going to where Flossie and Freddie were standing on boxes and reaching up into a low tree, told them if he caught them climbing up again he would send them both to the house.

"I didn't climb!" said Flossie, which was true enough.

"And I didn't climb very far, but I won't go up at all any more," declared Freddie.

The work of gathering the cherries on Red Gate Farm, as well as on the three other places near, was now in full swing. The orchards echoed with the talk, the laughter, the whistling and singing of the pickers. Every day auto trucks took crate after crate of the red cherries to the railroad station, not far away. These were then shipped to different cities.

Mr. Bobbsey had made arrangements with an agent in one city to take all the cherries he could ship, so there was no need of peddling the fruit around, as Bert had seen Nick Dodge doing for the truck farmer who had hired him. As for Nick, after that first glimpse of him up in a tree on Mr. Winton's farm, the unpleasant lad had not been seen by either Nan or Bert.

"He'd better keep out of my way—that's all!" said Bert. "If he throws any more mud I'll fix him!"

"You aren't sure he did it," Nan reminded her brother.

"I'm sure all I want to be!" answered Bert.

Tree after tree was stripped of its fruit, the cherries being picked with their stems on, as they keep better in this condition. Of course some cherries were pulled off without any stems—Flossie and Freddie were most likely to gather their fruit in this fashion—but such cherries were either sold around Cherry Corners or else made up into preserves by Dinah and Mrs. Bobbsey. They would not keep long, once they were pulled from their stems.

As Nan and Bert filled their pails or baskets, sometimes using one and again the other container, they carried them to the sorting shed where men and women, engaged by their father, looked over the fruit and arranged it nicely in quart baskets, the kind used for strawberries. These baskets were packed in crates, containing thirty-two quarts, fastened shut, and shipped away.

As might be expected, Flossie and Freddie soon grew tired of picking the fruit, and they also ate as much as was good for them.

Their mother, on a trip through the orchard, observing this, called to them:

"How would you like to ride to the station with me on the auto truck?"

"Oh, fine!" cried Freddie, dropping his pail.

"I'm coming, too!" screamed Flossie.

"I think I will, also, to help you look after them," said Nan, with a smile. "I'm tired of standing up on a ladder."

"Very well, my dear," said her mother. "I think it will be a good change for you. I wonder if Bert wants to come?"

But when Bert heard of the plan he said:

"Thanks, Mother, but I'm going to stay and pick cherries. I want to get money enough for a new fish pole."

So he remained with the other pickers, and, really, he did very well for a small boy. Several times his father had to warn him against climbing too high in the tree.

"Leave the high cherries for the men, they know better how to get them," said Mr. Bobbsey.

But Bert was eager, and once, forgetting what his father had told him, he moved his ladder to allow him to reach a part of the tree not yet picked, and climbed up.

Bert did not plant his ladder securely on the ground, and his weight shifted it. So when he had climbed toward the top and was reaching over to pull off some specially large, red cherries, he suddenly heard a cry below him of:

"Look out there, boy! You're slipping!"

It was the voice of one of the men pickers, and, even as Bert heard it, he realized that the ladder was slipping to one side and that he was going with it.

"Grab hold of a limb and hang on!" shouted the man below the boy, and Bert had sense enough to obey. His pail was fast to a limb near him by that S shaped wire hook, and with both hands Bert grasped the same branch.

There he clung, while the ladder, gliding along the leafy branches, fell over on its side, leaving Bert suspended in the air like a man on a circus trapeze.

"Hold fast! I'll have the ladder up to you in a minute!" cried the man on the ground, near whom the ladder had fallen. "Don't let go!"

"I won't!" answered Bert, who was a bit alarmed, though, as a matter of fact, the ground was not very far down and it was so thickly covered with grass that he might not have been hurt beyond a hard jolt or shaking up. But Bert did not want to fall, so he clung to the limb.

The man soon had the ladder raised again, having pushed the end up to where Bert could put his feet on it and thus take the strain off his arms, which, to tell the truth, were beginning to ache.

"You don't want to move a ladder all by yourself, youngster," warned the man when he had seen that the boy was all right. "They're tricky things—are ladders. Better call one of us the next time."

"I will, thank you," said the boy, and he was glad his father had not been there to see what happened. He might have stopped Bert from picking any more cherries. As it happened, however, no harm resulted and because Bert had his pail hanging in a tree branch and not on the ladder that fell, his cherries were not spilled.

The work was now going on well, men,

women, and boys filling their pails and baskets rapidly and carrying them to the sorting shed. Bert did this with his, and he saw with satisfaction that his "tickets" were mounting up.

Tickets were the slips of paper given out by the foreman whom Mr. Bobbsey had hired. Each ticket showed how many quarts of cherries had been picked by the person holding it, and Bert began to figure how many more tickets he would need to enable him to buy the new fishing rod.

"I've got to pick a lot more quarts, though," he told himself, as he again went back to his tree.

It was late afternoon when Mrs. Bobbsey took Nan, Flossie, and Freddie to the railroad station to see the crates of cherries being loaded into freight cars, the four riding on one of the auto trucks, and it was nearly supper time when they returned. The pickers were finishing their day's work, and some had already stopped. To get in the whole crop on all four farms would take about three weeks, as some cherries were late in ripening.

Flossie and Freddie, as well as Nan, could

hardly wait to get back to Red Gate Farm, for they had some wonderful news to tell Bert Bobbsey.

"What you think!" cried Freddie, as soon as he saw his brother.

"You'll never guess what's coming!" added Flossie.

"Christmas is coming!" said Bert, with a laugh.

"No, it's a circus train!" shouted Freddie, jumping up and down in his excitement. "A circus train!"

"With elephants and monkeys and everything!" added Flossie.

"A circus train?" repeated Bert, wonderingly.

"And we're going to see it!" said Freddie. "Oh, I wish it would come now!"

"It's coming to-morrow! The circus train is coming to-morrow!" sang Flossie.

CHAPTER XIV

A MISSING CAKE

QUESTIONINGLY Bert Bobbsey looked at his mother.

"Is a circus coming here?" he asked.

"Not the circus," she answered. "It wouldn't pay a big circus to stop at Cherry Corners, for not enough people would come to see it. But the ticket agent at the railroad station said a big circus train would pass through here to-morrow on its way to Denville."

"Over the railroad back of Red Gate Farm?" asked Bert. Some distance back of the cherry orchard were the shining iron rails on a high embankment of dirt and cinders.

"Yes, on our railroad," declared Freddie. as soon as he learned there was a railroad back of the farm his father had got, the "little fireman" spoke of it as "our railroad."

"And we're going to get up early and watch the train go through," added Flossie. "Aren't we, Mother?"

"I guess so," was the smiling answer. "You'll have to get up before breakfast, however."

"I always get up before breakfast!" announced Freddie. "That is, 'less I'm sick! And I'm not sick now and I'm glad of it, 'cause I want to see the elephants."

"I guess you won't see many elephants," Bert said. "They keep them in closed cars, and they do the same with all the other animals."

"Some of the cars have slats on them, like the crate we brought Snap here in," suggested Nan. "Maybe we can look through the slats and see some of the animals."

"Maybe," agreed Bert, who had not thought of this. "But are you going to let them get up to see the circus train come through?" he asked his mother, nodding at Flossie and Freddie.

"I thought perhaps, if you and Nan got up

early enough and wanted to walk back of the farm to see the train, you'd take Flossie and Freddie with you," suggested Mrs. Bobbsey.

"Oh, sure we will!" promised Bert. "It will be early—before the cherry picking starts, and I can come back as soon as the train goes on. Sure we'll go!"

This delighted the young twins, and they were soon talking of nothing but the chances of seeing some of the circus animals as the cars rumbled past Cherry Corners on the way to the city beyond.

Mrs. Bobbsey had learned from the station agent about what time the circus train was expected. It was an hour before Dinah would serve the Bobbsey breakfast, and Freddie was so afraid Bert might oversleep that he begged his mother to set the alarm clock, which was done.

The bell sounded its warning tinkle and Bert, awakened by it, could not for a few moments remember what it was all about. But soon Freddie excitedly whispered:

"Come on! We're going to see the circus train!"

A little later the four twins were on their

way over the back pasture and through a patch of woods on their way to the railroad tracks. Snap went with them, running here and there, sniffing and snuffing at holes in the ground, at stone fence corners where, once, he surprised a chipmunk, and again at a hollow tree, where some big animal seemed to be hiding.

"Maybe it's a bear!" suggested Freddie. "A circus bear!"

"The circus train isn't here yet, so how could it be a bear?" asked Flossie.

Freddie did not answer, for just then a whistle sounded, and he cried:

"Here comes the circus train now!"

"Let's hurry!" begged Nan, and Bert, calling to Snap to leave off sniffing around the hollow log, hastened on with the smaller children.

When they emerged from the woods the railroad embankment was in sight, and around a curve rolled a long train of gay red and yellow cars. Some of the cars were flat, and on them were the brilliant circus wagons. Most of them, however, were covered with big pieces of canvas to keep off any rain, and so not much of a view could be had of the chariots, except in places where the covering was torn.

Reaching a safe place, and one where a good view could be had, Bert and his brother and sisters watched the circus train rumble past. Several pickers from Red Gate Farm had gotten up early to come out and view the sight, and there were also men and boys who worked on the other three farms.

The railroad went up a grade back of Red Gate Farm, and because the circus train was heavy, the engines could not pull it very fast. The slow movement gave the Bobbsey children and the others a good chance to view the circus cars.

"Oh, I see an elephant!" suddenly cried Flossie, pointing to one car, the sides of which were made of heavy slats. And, sure enough, as this car came opposite to the children an elephant thrust its trunk out of a wide crack.

"Oh, I wish he'd come all the way out." cried Freddie.

"Look!" exclaimed Nan, pointing to another car. "I see some zebras!" and she indicated these prettily striped animals to the others.

Then followed a number of cars, gay in red, blue, yellow, and gold paint, some with mirrors in gilt frames on their sides. But what was in them, whether animals or circus tents, the children did not know.

The train was a long one, and rumbled on up the small hill. Then Bert heard a boy, whom he had seen picking cherries on Mr. Tansy's farm, remark:

"The train'll stop in a minute."

"How do you know?" asked another lad and, hearing a voice he knew, Bert turned and saw Nick Dodge standing near. But Nick did not seem to see Bert. At least, he paid no attention to him or the other Bobbsey children.

"How do you know the train's going to stop?" asked Nick again.

"Because all trains stop at the top of the hill to get water for the engines," answered the other boy. "There's a water tank there."

"Do you think the train will stop, Bert?" asked Freddie, who had heard what Nick asked.

"I don't know. I suppose so," was the answer.

A moment later the hard puffing of the locomotives (there were two on the train) came to an end and the cars slowly rumbled to a halt. The first engine was taking water, or rather, the tender behind it was having its tank filled.

"Oh, now we can see everything fine!" cried Flossie.

However, there really was not much to see, for when the train stopped the cars opposite to the Bobbsey twins contained only horses, and these were not much of a novelty. But Flossie and Freddie, at least, were thrilled.

"Maybe when the train goes on," suggested Freddie, "we'll see cars with lions and tigers in 'em!"

"I hope none of 'em get loose!" murmured Flossie.

"Don't worry! None of them will get out," replied Nan.

Bert now observed Nick Dodge climbing up the railroad bank, and the boy who was with him called:

"What you going to do?"

"Get on one of the circus cars," was the answer.

"You don't dare!"

"Pooh! I never take a dare!" cried Nick, and then, to the surprise of Bert and the others, they saw the boy climb up the side of a red and yellow car that was coupled behind one containing a number of ponies, which could be seen through the slats. The car on which Nick climbed was closed on all sides, but it contained several windows, over which were heavy wooden shutters.

"What's in that car?" called the boy who was with Nick.

"Don't know. But I'm going to find out!" was the reply.

Bert, Nan, and the smaller twins saw Nick fumbling with an iron bar across one of the wooden shutters.

"You'd better be careful!" warned the other lad. "If any of the circus men catch you——"

"Pooh! Who's afraid?" sneered Nick, and suddenly he loosed the bar and the shutter dropped down, being hinged at the bottom.

"Oh, now you did it!" shouted Nick's companion.

"Look, Bert!" whispered Freddie.

"Hush!" warned Nan. "We don't want to get into a quarrel with that boy."

Nick, in spite of his boast that he was not afraid, seemed a bit alarmed at the result of his prank. He tried to reach down to pull up the shutter again, but could not.

"Any animals in there?" asked the other boy.

Before Nick could answer, another cherry picker, a lad from the farm where Nick worked, cried:

"Look out! The train's going to start!"

Two sharp whistles sounded from the engine at the water tank. Nick began a scramble to reach the ground, and did so before the train actually got going. There was a loud clatter as the heavy circus cars yanked at their couplings, and then an iron grating that was fastened inside the window the shutter of which Nick had loosened swung back. Several animals appeared at the opening thus unexpectedly made.

"Oh, look! Monkeys!" shouted Freddie.

"Monkeys! Monkeys!" echoed Flossie.

"That's right!" agreed Bert, as he and Nan saw several of the monkeys putting their paws and queer faces out of the window.

"Look what you did, Nick!" said one of the lads with him. "You'll let those animals out."

"Maybe there are bears and lions in that car, too," added another lad.

"No, there ain't!" said Nick, who had rejoined his companions. "There are only monkeys in that car. I looked in. I guess they won't get out. Anyhow, I don't care if they do. Nobody will know I opened the window unless you fellows tell."

"We won't tell!" promised the two older lads, and Nick looked over toward Bert, but he said nothing to the Bobbsey boy.

The train was once more on its way, but aside from several monkeys, one or two of them quite large, who thrust their tails, paws, or heads out of the window, nothing seemed likely to happen.

"I guess it's all right," said Nick, and he seemed relieved that his mischievous trick would have no ill results. The train puffed its way on up the grade, and then came to a stop again.

"Oh, maybe they have found out some of the animals are going to get loose!" suggested Flossie.

"I guess nothing like that will happen," said Bert. "Though that window in the monkey car ought to be closed."

"The other engine's getting water now," called a boy who was farther up the track, and this was what was taking place. When the tender of the one locomotive was filled, it pulled ahead, out of the way, so the other one could be filled. When this was done the circus train resumed its way in earnest.

The last of the red, yellow, gold, and mirrored cars passed before the eyes of the Bobbsey twins, and then the excitement was over for the day.

"I wish the circus was going to stay here," sighed Freddie. "I'd like to see some of the elephants—I mean a whole elephant—not just his trunk."

"I'd like to see some monkeys!" echoed

Flossie. "Maybe some will get out," she added hopefully.

"I guess not," remarked Bert, with a laugh. "And now I'm going back and pick cherries," he added. "I want to get enough money to buy my new fish pole."

The other boys, and some men who had come to see the circus train, also began to leave, and soon the Bobbsey twins were eating breakfast, which Dinah, listening with wide-eyed wonder to the tales Flossie and Freddie told her of what they had seen, served.

The weather was fine, and the cherries were ripening nicely, which made the four farms busy places of work. Mr. Bobbsey was delighted with his cherry crop, and said he hoped to make a goodly sum by the sale of the fruit.

"If the rain holds off we'll do exceedingly well!" he said to his wife.

"Can't we pick cherries in the rain?" asked Bert.

"Well, you could pick them, yes," answered his father. "But wet cherries are not good to pack and send away. They rot too quickly. We need dry weather."

The sun continued to shine, which was a good thing. Merrily the cherry picking went on. There were one or two accidents. Once a boy on Mr. Winton's farm fell out of a tree and broke his arm, and was taken to the doctor's office to have it set. Another time a ladder slipped and fell on a stack of crates filled with cherries on Mr. Bobbsey's place, smashing into pulp several quarts of the fruit. Once when Bert had filled a large pail and was coming down off the ladder with it, he slipped and, to save himself, had to let go the pail. His cherries spilled on the ground and he lost several quarts of them, not being allowed to turn in the crushed fruit.

But nothing more serious happened, and everything went very well. The Bobbsey twins were glad they had come to Cherry Corners and Bert was very industrious, not letting a day pass that he did not earn some money. Nan also picked, but she wanted to learn to be a housekeeper, so spent much time in the kitchen with Dinah and her mother.

Two days after the circus train had passed through, Nan baked a chocolate cake. It was a fine one of several layers, with thick chocolate in between.

"Set it out on de back porch to cool," Dinah advised, and Nan did so. She had promised Bert a piece of the cake if it turned out well, and it had, so Nan was anxious for her brother to see the result of her efforts.

After about an hour she decided that the cake was cool enough to set away in the pantry, and she went to the back porch to get it.

"What's de mattah, honey lamb?" asked Dinah, who heard Nan utter a startled cry.

"My cake! My lovely chocolate cake! It's gone!" wailed Nan. "Oh, dear! My chocolate cake is gone!"

CHAPTER XV

A STRANGE ALARM

HAVING finished his cherry picking for that day, Bert Bobbsey came up to the farmhouse in time to hear Nan's sad voice.

"What's the matter?" he asked.

"Somebody took the chocolate cake I just baked and set out here to cool!" was the answer.

"They did?" exclaimed Bert. "That was a funny thing to do!"

"I call it a mean trick!" cried Nan.

"Took yo' cake, did dey, honey?" muttered Dinah, as she waddled out to where Nan was explaining matters to her brother. "Whar am de rascal? I'll done fix him! Whar am he?"

"Oh, I didn't see any one take it," Nan made haste to explain. "I just came out here and it was gone."

"Are you sure you put it here?" Bert asked.

"Why, of course I'm sure!" declared Nan. "What do you mean?"

"Well, I mean sometimes you put things down and forget where you laid them," explained Bert. "Oh, I do the same thing myself," he hastened to say, as he noted Nan's cheeks flushing.

"This wasn't like that at all," retorted Bert's sister. "I baked the cake and carried it out here. Dinah saw me!"

"'Deed an' I did!" asserted the colored cook.

"Besides, you can see the rim of the pan," resumed Nan. "And look, Bert, here are some cake crumbs!"

The evidence was too plain to be mistaken. There was a slightly greasy rim on the bench —a rim made by the pan on which Nan had set her cake after putting chocolate between the layers and on top. And there were fresh crumbs.

"I know who took that cake!" suddenly exclaimed Bert.

"You do? Who was it?" demanded Nan.

"That Nick Dodge! He sneaked up here and took it to eat—him and some of those other pickers that were with him to see the circus train."

"Did you see him?" asked Nan.

"No. But I'll bet he took it. It would be just like him!"

"Oh, if you didn't see him, you can't be sure he took it," and Nan's voice showed disappointment.

"No, and you mustn't say Nick took it unless you are positive," put in Mrs. Bobbsey, who had come into the kitchen in time to hear what had happened. "Are you sure, Bert?"

"No, Mother, I'm not sure. But——"

"Then don't say it," she warned him. "It may have been anybody else. While Nick is mischievous and tricky, we must not accuse him wrongly."

"I'm going over there and find out if he did take it!" declared Bert, starting in the direction of Mr. Winton's house, where Nick boarded, together with other cherry pickers.

"No, Bert! Don't do that!" advised his mother. "There has been trouble enough with that boy. You cannot even suggest that he took the chocolate cake unless you have some good reason."

But there was none, except Bert's idea that it was just the kind of trick Nick would play, and so the matter had to be dropped. The lovely cake Nan had made had just mysteriously vanished. Flossie and Freddie, who had been playing back of the farmhouse, were questioned, but said they had seen no boys sneaking around as if on the lookout for an unexpected treat.

"Maybe the birds ate the cake!" suggested Flossie.

"If it had been birds they would have picked up all the crumbs," declared Nan. "They wouldn't have left these big ones," and she pointed to several rather large pieces of cake on the bench.

"It's just as if a fellow grabbed the cake up quickly and ran off with it," said Bert, and that was how it seemed to all.

However, the cake was gone, and there was no use trying to find it, though Flossie and Freddie wandered about the back yard and the orchard, hoping they might discover it.

Luckily, Dinah had made a pie while Nan was baking her cake, so there was dessert for supper, after all.

That night there was a lovely full moon and it was so pleasant that Mrs. Bobbsey allowed even Flossie and Freddie to sit up later than usual on the porch before going to bed. Mr. Bobbsey was there, talking to his wife about the cherry crop.

"It's the largest in many years," he said. "We came to Red Gate Farm just in time."

"The children are having a lovely vacation," said their mother. "It is doing them good."

"And I've got enough now for my new fish pole," announced Bert. "I like picking cherries."

"It's hard work, but I like it, too," said Nan. "I'm going to start picking again to-morrow."

"You'll have to be lively!" her father warned her. "The cherry season will not last forever, and though there are a number of trees of late ones that will soon be ready, most of my crop is already gathered."

"If you would let me climb high up in the

trees I could pick more cherries," said Freddie.

"You had one accident in a tree," warned his mother, "and we don't want any more. And now I think it's time you two were in bed."

The smaller twins protested at this and begged for a little more time, which was allowed them, and then, yawning and trying to keep their eyes open, but insisting that they were not in the least sleepy, they went upstairs.

About an hour later the rest of the family followed and soon the farmhouse was quiet with the silvery moon shining down on it.

But about midnight, or perhaps an hour afterward, Mrs. Bobbsey was awakened in her room, which was across from the one where Freddie was sleeping alone, for he and Flossie were now considered large enough to have beds to themselves.

"Mother! Mother!" murmured Freddie in a half-sleepy voice.

"What is it, dear? Do you want a drink?" she asked, for this was frequently the cause of awakening on the part of the younger twins.

"No, I don't want a drink," Freddie answered. Then he cried out as if in terror:

"There's somebody in my room!"

His voice was so excited that it alarmed his mother, who hurriedly left her bed and crossed the hall, saying:

"Nonsense! No one could be in your room. You are just having a funny dream, Freddie."

But when she reached him she found him sitting up in bed, and the light she turned on showed his eyes wide in wonder and some alarm. He pointed to the open window.

"Something came in there!" he declared. "I saw it in the moonlight."

"What was it like?" asked Mr. Bobbsey, who had joined his wife in Freddie's room.

"It was like a dog," declared the little boy. "I guess maybe it was Snap trying to get in to sleep in my bed," and he laughed when he said this, for he loved Snap.

"Yes, perhaps it was Snap," said Mr. Bobbsey, at the same time he made a signal to his wife to say nothing more. To Freddie he added: "Now go to sleep again. I'll go down and chain Snap up so he won't bother you again."

"Oh, he didn't bother me—I like Snap to come into my room," went on Freddie. "But he looked so funny there on my window sill in the moonlight," and the little boy laughed. He was no longer alarmed, but turned over and was asleep almost as soon as his head lay back on the pillow.

"How could Snap climb up the side of the house and get in Freddie's window?" whispered Mrs. Bobbsey to her husband when they were out of Freddie's room.

"The dog didn't climb up," was the answer. "Freddie just had a dream, but I let him think it was Snap. That was the best way to quiet him."

"It might have been Snap, though. Better take a look and see where he is." And when it was found that the dog was lying out in front of his kennel, Mr. and Mrs. Bobbsey knew it could not have been the children's pet that caused the night alarm.

"I suppose it was a dream," said Mrs. Bobbsey, as she went back to bed.

But that was not the end of the night

disturbance. About two hours later Flossie gave a wailing cry, and when her mother hurried into the room the little girl pointed to her open window and exclaimed:

"A big cat came in there. He wanted to get in my bed, but I threw one of my shoes at him. I don't like cats to get on my bed, except maybe Snoop, and he isn't up here. It was a brown cat, not a black one."

"Nonsense, dear," soothed her mother. "There has been no cat in your room."

"Yes there has!" insisted Flossie. "I saw him on my window sill, and I threw my shoe at him when he jumped to come on my bed. Look, there's my shoe by the window now."

And, sure enough, when the light was turned up, one of Flossie's shoes was in the middle of the room, halfway between her bed and the window. The other shoe, with her stockings nicely folded, was near the chair that contained her garments.

"She did throw it," said Mrs. Bobbsey.

"She, too, must have been dreaming," remarked Mr. Bobbsey.

"It is rather strange they should both be

dreaming about animals coming into their rooms," said Mrs. Bobbsey, as she and her husband went out, having calmed Flossie so that she turned over to go to sleep again.

"It is, rather," admitted Mr. Bobbsey. "I'll have a look around outside."

But he saw nothing, and told his wife so.

"Perhaps it was shadows cast by the trees in the moonlight," said Mrs. Bobbsey, as the house settled down to quiet again.

There was no further excitement that night, and in the morning Freddie and Flossie forgot about the strange alarms, for they were to go on a picnic with their mother that day, to eat their lunch in the woods, and this always pleased them.

Dinah was also to go along. The colored cook objected at first, saying she had too much work to do. But as Mr. Bobbsey had engaged another cook to look after the cherry pickers, who slept and ate in a small house some distance away from the main one, there really was no reason why Dinah could not go to the picnic.

"We'll leave something for Bert and Mr. Bobbsey to eat, and we'll take a day off," said Mrs. Bobbsey, and so it was arranged. Bert and his father had a busy day before them, as some of the cherries were ripening faster than had been expected. They found their lunch set out for them in Dinah's kitchen, and, after eating it, again went back to the orchard.

It was when Dinah, Mrs. Bobbsey, Nan, and the smaller twins returned to the house that something else was found to have happened. The colored cook took one look inside the room where she held sway and excitedly cried:

"Oh, look what done took place in mah kitchen! Oh, what a mess! Somebody's been cuttin' up in heah!"

CHAPTER XVI

BERT'S WATCH

Certainly there was a mess in Dinah's kitchen. Pots and pans were strewed about the floor, the drawers of the table and dish closet were open, and some cups and saucers had been broken. A loaf of bread seemed to have been crumbled into bits and the pieces tossed about, and where Dinah had put away a choice pie for supper, now only the empty pan was left.

"Who did all this?" exclaimed Freddie, as he looked in the upset kitchen.

Bert and his father came to look in, having heard the exclamations of dismay.

"It was some boys who did this!" declared Nan. "It's just the work of some bad boys!"

"It couldn't have been Snap," said Mrs. Bobbsey. "He was with us all afternoon."

"It was a boy, all right!" insisted Bert. "And I think I know which one."

"You mean Nick?" asked Nan.

"That's the fellow! I'm going over where he is and——"

"Better go slow, son," advised Mr. Bobbsey. "There is no way of being certain that Nick Dodge did this. But surely these dishes never got broken by themselves, nor did the pie walk off. I will make some inquiries of the other farmers around here and see if they know whether any of their cherry pickers were away at the time when this might have been done. Let me ask some questions before you accuse Nick of having done this."

"Ef I lay mah hands on de boy whut done dis," muttered Dinah, "I'll smear him wif molasses an put him inside a beehive, dat's whut I'll do!"

"That would be severe punishment," agreed Mrs. Bobbsey. "But we must first catch the boy."

With the help of Mrs. Bobbsey and Nan,

the fat cook soon got the kitchen in order again, while Bert and Mr. Bobbsey looked about for something that might tell what boy or boys did the mischief.

"I think it was more than one boy," said the children's father.

"That Nick has a couple of fellows he goes around with," remarked Bert. "They could easily have done it."

But when Mr. Bobbsey asked Mr. Winton, for whom Nick worked, if that lad had been away from the cherry orchard any time during the afternoon when Dinah's kitchen was upset, the farmer replied:

"I hardly think he was. You see, I'm rushing my pickers now, on account of the fruit ripening faster than I counted on, and I told every one of them that for the next two days I'd give a quarter of a cent more a quart than I've been paying. So every one of them stuck pretty close to work. I don't believe any of the boys here sneaked off to make mischief in your kitchen. But I'll scout around and see if I can find out."

Two or three days passed, but there was no further news about Nick or any other boy who might have played the mean trick on Dinah, and Bert had to admit that he could not prove anything against the former truck peddler's boy.

"If we said he did it," stated Mr. Bobbsey, "he would just tell us he didn't, and we would be no better off than before."

In spite of this, however, Bert was sure Nick was to blame, not only for the trouble in the kitchen, but for the mud ball that had hit him.

"I'm going to keep watch on Nick!" declared the elder Bobbsey lad.

This, however, was easier said than done. For Bert was kept busy picking cherries, and so was Nick. Consequently the two boys saw very little of each other. Once or twice Bert worked extra hard and picked his usual quantity of fruit by early afternoon. He then slipped away and hid in the bushes near Mr. Winton's farm.

From this hiding place Bert watched Nick. But though the other lad sneaked away from the orchard several times when he was supposed to remain and pick, and though Bert saw Nick playing tricks on other pickers, yet there was nothing that pointed to the lad as the one who had caused the mischief on the Bobbsey farm.

But instead of the annoying little tricks coming to an end, they increased in number, and it did not appear that Nick could be blamed for all of them.

Once, when Bert was taking a short cut through the woods, going to the village store on an errand for his mother, he was struck on the head by a stick that fell out of a tree. It was only a light branch and did not hurt him, but when Bert saw the stick he knew it had been thrown at him, and had not fallen.

"For it was a newly broken branch," Bert told his father. "Somebody up in the tree twisted it off and threw it down at me."

"Did you see any one?" Mr. Bobbsey asked.

"No," Bert replied. "But I saw the branches jiggling just as if some one were up in them."

"It is curious," said the lumber merchant, looking at the limb Bert handed him. "As you say, it isn't a dead branch that might have fallen naturally. It was broken off and tossed down."

Another time Nan had taken Flossie and Freddie down to a shady place at the end of the garden to amuse them. Nan took a doll with her, as did Flossie, while Freddie had his toy engine. The little fireman went to the brook to fill his tank with water and remained there playing, but not far away from his sisters.

Nan and Flossie put the dolls to "sleep" and then walked off a little way to dabble their toes in the water. When the girls returned the dolls had been roughly pulled from their beds in the grass and the dress of Flossie's doll was torn off.

"Oh, who did this?" cried Nan, when she saw what had happened.

"Just look at my Clarabell! Standing on her head and her dress gone!" wailed Flossie. "It was Freddie who did this!"

But Freddie was playing at the brook with his engine, and he was so earnest in saying he had not been near the dolls that his sisters must believe him. Besides, Freddie never played mean tricks like that, and it was mean to tear the dress off the doll.

"I don't like it here!" murmured Flossie, looking nervously around the bushes. "Let's go home!"

When the children told what had taken place, Mrs. Bobbsey was more than ever mystified about the strange things that were happening at Cherry Corners.

"It must be some tricky boys," she declared. "I think your father will have to tell the police."

When the next thing happened, Mr. Bobbsey, too, decided that the police ought to be called in. For Bert, going up to his room to dress for supper after a hard day at picking cherries, called downstairs:

"Has any one seen my silver watch?"

"It was on your bureau a little while ago," answered Nan. "I saw it when I went in to turn back your bed covers."

"Well, my watch isn't on my bureau now!" exclaimed Bert. "It's gone! That Nick Dodge must have climbed up the rain-water pipe, got in a window, and taken my silver watch! Where's Dad?"

CHAPTER XVII

IN THE MUD HOLE

BERT'S silver watch had been a birthday present, and he thought a great deal of it. So when he found it was missing from his bureau, though it had been there earlier in the day, he was angry.

"I'm going to tell Dad about it," he declared to Nan, who met him in the hall. "That is, unless you hid my watch for fun," and he looked at his sister.

"I wouldn't do a thing like that!" declared Nan.

"No, I guess you wouldn't," answered Bert. "I wonder if Freddie took it?"

"What would he want of your watch, Bert Bobbsey?"

"He might think he could take some of the wheels out to use in his fire engine."

"Bert Bobbsey!" cried Nan. "Freddie wouldn't do such a thing!"

"I know it! I was only joking when I said that," Bert went on. "But maybe Freddie did see my watch."

However, when the "little fireman" was questioned he said he had not been in Bert's room all day. Nor had Dinah nor Mr. or Mrs. Bobbsey seen the silver time-piece.

"Perhaps you mislaid it," suggested Bert's mother. "More than once you have said you couldn't find a clean handkerchief or a pair of stockings when I told you just where they were. You would say they weren't in the drawer, when there they were, all the while. Perhaps your watch is on your bureau, under the cover or hidden behind your comb and brush."

"No, Mother, it isn't! I looked!" declared Bert.

"I'll go up and help you," offered Nan, but her bright eyes were of no avail. The watch was not to be found, and finally Mrs. Bobbsey had to admit that it was not in the room. Bert's father suggested his son might have worn the watch while picking cherries, and have dropped it from his pocket.

"No, I didn't have it on to-day!" declared the boy.

"And I saw it on his bureau when I went in to open his bed for the night," said Nan again, which made it certain that the silver watch had disappeared that afternoon.

"Nick must have taken it!" insisted Bert again. "He could easily have climbed by the rain-water pipe to the shed roof and have gotten in my window that way. The bureau is close to the window, and he could reach his hand in and take my watch."

"This is a serious matter," remarked Mr. Bobbsey. "More serious than throwing mud balls or sticks, or even upsetting Dinah's kitchen. We must not accuse a boy of stealing unless we know for sure."

"Hadn't we better tell the police?" asked Bert. "I want to get my watch back."

"I think I will make a report of it," decided Mr. Bobbsey. "They have no regular police here in Cherry Corners, but there is a constable. I'll tell him and see what he says about it. I will also speak of Bert's watch to the owners of the three other cherry farms around here, and have them keep their eyes open to see if any of the pickers has a new silver watch."

But though his father was thus proceeding in an orderly way, Bert decided he would do something himself. This was to keep a careful lookout over Nick Dodge, to see if that lad showed any of his chums the missing watch.

By this time Bert had picked enough cherries to earn the money to buy the fishing rod he wanted, and he was not quite so eager to gather the fruit as he had been at first. Mr. Bobbsey had plenty of regular pickers, and did not really need the services of his son. He had only let him pick to give him an idea of business and to know what it felt like to really earn money.

So, without saying anything to his parents, Bert decided to play amateur detective. He told Nan of his plans and made her promise not to tell.

"I'll just hang around Mr. Winton's orchard," decided Bert, "and when I see Nick stopping his work I'll follow him and see where he goes. Maybe I'll see him taking my watch out to look at it."

"What will you do then?" Nan wanted to know.

"I'll take it away from him."

"Maybe he won't let you!"

"Then he'll have a fight on his hands!' declared Bert fiercely. "I'm not going tc let him keep my birthday watch."

"Maybe he won't let you follow him," went on Nan, who, though anxious to have her brother get back his timepiece, wanted him to understand all the troubles he might meet.

"I won't let him know I'm following him," whispered Bert. "I'll sneak along through the bushes behind him, just as we do when we play scout and Indians. He'll never know I'm following him."

"If he does, there'll be a fuss," declared Nan, and that is just what happened.

Carrying out his plan, Bert gave up for a time his cherry picking and found a place at the side of the road near the particular trees where Mr. Winton's fruit was being gathered at this time. Nick and the other helpers were up in the trees there, and Bert, by "scouting around," as he called it, found the very tree which Nick Dodge was in.

About the middle of the afternoon Bert saw Nick take his big pail of cherries to the sorting shed to be measured, and then he heard the lad say:

"I'm going to quit for the day. I'm going fishing."

"All right—you've done pretty well," said the man in charge of the orchard. "Will you be here to-morrow?"

"Oh, sure! I'm going to stick here until there aren't any more cherries to pick. I like this better than peddling vegetables," went on Nick.

"This is my chance!" whispered Bert to himself. "I'll follow him when he goes fishing."

A little later Nick came out of the shack where he and the other men pickers on Mr. Winton's farm lived during the busy season. Nick had a pole over his shoulder.

"I hope he doesn't go to my fishing hole," thought Bert. "He'd only spoil it. But I guess he won't find it."

Bert had a special little nook of his own where he went to fish, and he was anxious to keep it secret. However, Nick did not appear to know about it, for he headed in the opposite direction, and Bert followed, though at a distance.

"He doesn't know I'm after him!" murmured Nan's brother. "It's a good thing I practiced being an Indian, because now I can walk through the woods without making any noise."

This is not exactly true, but Bert did manage to slip along back of Nick without, it would seem, that lad's knowing anything about it. Nick crossed through a patch of woods and was soon nearing the small river which lazily wended its way about Cherry Corners in a big half circle.

"If he's got my watch with him," reasoned Bert, as he slipped from one tree to another in the chase, "he'll take it out after a while to see what time it is. Then I'll rush up and grab it."

For half an hour Nick trudged on without taking out any watch. By this time he was close to the river, and Bert was wondering what would happen when he got to the open fields on the edge of the stream.

"I can't stand up and walk then," decided the Bobbsey boy. "I'll have to crawl on my hands and knees in the tall grass."

Nick reached the end of the woods and began to cross the field, beyond which lay the little river. Bert hesitated a moment, and then, dropping to his hands and knees, followed.

Whether it was some noise made by Bert, or whether Nick turned and saw the waving grass as Bert crawled through it, does not matter. What happened was that suddenly Bert heard him cry:

"Who's there? Who's following me?"

Before Bert could answer a stick sailed through the air, thrown by Nick, and struck the Bobbsey lad on the back.

"Take that!" cried Nick.

At this Bert lost his temper, for the blow was a smart one, and, leaping to his feet, he rushed forward, shouting:

"I'm following you, and you know what for! Give it up! Give it back to me!"

Without stopping to say what it was he

wanted, Bert rushed at the surprised Nick. At that moment the other lad was standing on the edge of the river, at a low place where there were several mud holes.

Hardly knowing what he was doing, Bert reached the side of his enemy, and, with a vigorous shove, pushed him down the bank into the slimy mud and water. Into this Nick fell with a great splash.

CHAPTER XVIII

NICK'S TRICK

SURPRISED at the unexpected success of his attack on the larger boy, Bert Bobbsey stood for a moment on the edge of the bank, looking down at the struggling Nick Dodge. For Nick splashed about and struggled as he fell.

"I guess that wasn't a very good thing to do if Nick has my watch in his pocket," thought Bert. "It'll be all mud and water and rust. I wish I'd taken the watch out before I pushed him in."

But there was no time to think of this now, for Nick was very angry and Bert knew his enemy would rush at him as soon as he could emerge from the mud hole. Never had Nick Dodge been so furious. He fairly glared up at Bert and yelled:

"I'll fix you for this!"

"You'll have to catch me first!" taunted Bert.

"What do you mean—shoving me into a mud hole like this?" went on Nick, as he wiped some of the dirt off his face and started to wade out. He had dropped his fishing pole in his fall.

"Give me back my watch that you took and I won't shove you down any more holes," said Bert.

"What do you mean—your watch? I haven't got it!"

"You have so!"

"I have not!"

"Didn't you climb up to our shed roof and get in my window and take my silver watch off my bureau?" asked Bert.

"No, I didn't! I never saw your old watch! But some of your friends will see a black eye on you as soon as I get out!" threatened Nick.

He spoke so earnesly about the watch that Bert thought perhaps, after all, he might be mistaken in thinking the truck peddler's boy had been guilty.

"Well, anyhow," went on Bert, "you threw a mud ball at me and you dropped a stick on me in the woods the other day. This pays back for those tricks!"

"I never dropped a stick on you in the woods!" declared Nick.

"You did! And you plopped the mud ball at me, too!"

"Well, I didn't hit you with any stick," went on Nick, which was almost as much as admitting that he had thrown the mud. "The only time I hit you with a stick was just now, when I threw one in the grass, and I didn't know you were there," went on Nick. "And I'm coming out now and black your eye and hit your nose!" he declared.

"I'm not afraid of you!" announced Bert, and he watched while the larger boy scrambled up the muddy bank. Bert did not want to run, yet he knew he would get considerably mussed up if he fought with Nick now.

Not only was Nick somewhat larger than Bert, but he was covered with water, mud, and green scum from the puddle into which he had been knocked. And Bert felt that much of this would rub off on his clothes if he got into a tussle with Nick.

"But I can't run away!" thought the Bobbsey lad.

However, the matter was solved for him. As Nick was climbing up the side of the river bank, to come at Bert, the larger lad stepped in a wet and slippery place and went down again into the mud—in he went deeper than before and he gave a howl of rage and disappointment.

"This is my chance to get away!" decided Bert. "I won't have to run, either," he added to himself. So he called down to the spluttering and splashing lad:

"I'm going home now. If you didn't take my watch you messed up Dinah's kitchen and you took Nan's chocolate cake and you daubed me with mud and now we're square!"

"Hey! Wait a minute! You wait and I'll fight you," offered Nick. "And I never was in your kitchen and I don't know anything about your sister's chocolate cake. If you aren't afraid you'll wait until I get out and I'll fight you!"

"I haven't time to wait now," said Bert.

"You might slip in again. I'm going home, and you want to keep away from our house, too!"

What Nick answered, Bert did not hear, for the Bobbsey lad turned and started back toward Cherry Corners, quite satisfied with what he had done to his enemy. It was not the right way to act, but Bert was human, and like many other boys, impulsive.

"If Nick didn't take my watch, who did?" mused Bert to himself as he trudged along. He listened now and then to see if he was being pursued, but no sounds came to his ears. "And if he didn't mess up Dinah's kitchen and take Nan's cake, who did?"

These were questions Bert very much wanted to have answered, but there seemed no way of finding out. Some very queer things were happening at Red Gate Farm, and if Nick Dodge was not doing the tricks, who was?

Thinking over these matters, wondering what would next happen, thinking of the new fishing rod he was going to buy with his cherry money, and rather worrying over what would take place when he next met Nick Dodge, Bert hurried back to the farmhouse.

"Why, Bert! what's the matter?" asked his mother, who was going for a walk with Flossie and Freddie.

"Nothing is the matter," replied the boy.

"Yes, there is, too!" exclaimed Nan, who was coming along the path behind her mother. "I can tell by your face, Bert Bobbsey, that something happened. Did you catch a big fish and did it get away?" and she laughed.

"Nothing like that," murmured Bert, wondering how his mother and sister could tell that something out of the ordinary had occurred.

"Have you been fighting?" asked Mrs Bobbsey.

"If he has, it was with that Nick Dodge!" declared Nan.

"I didn't exactly fight with him," admitted Bert, knowing it was best to tell the truth, as he always did. "I just pushed him into a mud hole after he hit me with a stick!"

"Oh, dear, I wish you hadn't!" murmured his mother. "It is going to make matters very unpleasant!"

"I guess it wasn't very pleasant for him to

be in the mud, but he deserved it. He threw a mud ball at me!" declared Bert.

Then he told the story, just as it had happened, how he had followed Nick to see if the other boy had the missing watch.

"I guess he didn't take it, after all," concluded Nan's brother, while Mrs. Bobbsey advised her son to go and tell his father all about it, since Mr. Bobbsey had begun to make some inquiries of the police about what had happened at Red Gate Farm.

"Are you going to pick any more cherries to-day, Bert?" asked Freddie, as his brother moved off toward the house. "If you are, I'll come and help you."

"Thanks, but I guess I won't pick any more until to-morrow," was the answer. "Where you going, Mother?"

"Just for a walk with the children. You may come if you like after you tell Daddy what happened."

"No, thank you," answered Bert after a moment's thought. "I guess I'll stay here until you come back."

He imagined he might meet Nick, wet and

muddy, coming along the road, and it would not be a very pleasant meeting.

"I'll let him have time to cool off," decided Bert.

However, nothing happened that night nor the next day. If Nick was anxious to meet Bert to fight with him, the boy gave no sign of it, but kept out of the way. Bert had an idea that Nick must have had to go in swimming with all his clothes on to get cleaned of the mud.

It was Mrs. Bobbsey who gave the next alarm about something happening in the farmhouse. She came downstairs one morning after breakfast, having gone up to dress in order to drive the auto to the village to buy some groceries.

"Did you take my cameo pin, Nan?" asked the girl's mother.

"Why, no, Mother!" Nan answered. "I haven't been in your room."

"My pin is gone," went on Mrs. Bobbsey. "I saw it on my dresser when I went down to breakfast, and I thought I would leave it out of my box, as I was going to wear it later. Now I can't find it."

"I didn't take it!" volunteered Flossie, who thought she would next be asked. "And Freddie didn't either! Did you?" and she turned to her brother.

"No, I haven't been in your room at all—not since you got the sliver out of my finger yesterday," said the little "fireman."

"It is very strange," murmured the children's mother. "First Bert's watch is taken and now my pin! I really think we have a very unpleasant sort of person in the neighborhood, who slips in and takes things when we are not looking. My cameo pin was not very valuable, nor was Bert's watch. But it isn't nice to lose things."

"I hope they don't take my bracelet!" exclaimed Nan. "I think I'll hide it," and she looked around apprehensively.

"I'm going to hide my best doll, too," added Flossie.

"My—my fire engine!" gasped Freddie. "If anybody takes that I'll—I'll—squirt water on 'em!" he threatened.

"How can you, if they take your engine?" asked Bert, who sometimes liked to tease his little brother.

"I'll throw water on 'em out of a pail and make 'em tell me where my engine is!" declared Freddie.

"I wish I could do that about my watch," said Bert. "Something will have to be done if things keep on like this."

"Maybe," suggested Freddie, "that funny dog I saw in my room the other night took your pin, Mother."

"Or the cat I saw," added Flossie.

Their mother shook her head. This was the first time the children had spoken of the animals that had alarmed them.

"I don't really believe you saw anything," Mrs. Bobbsey said.

"Yes, I did!" insisted Freddie.

"So did I!" added his twin sister.

Mr. Bobbsey could not account for what was happening. But then he was very busy attending to the cherries and had so many other things about which to think that he might be excused. But Bert and Nan wondered a great deal.

It was a day later that Dinah missed a bright new pan from her kitchen—a pan she intended to use in making a pudding.

"Freddie!" called out the fat black cook, "did yo' take mah pan to make mud pies?"

"No, Dinah! I didn't," he answered. "I haven't made any mud pies."

"Whar am mah other honey lamb?" went on Dinah, meaning Flossie. "Mebby she done tuck mah pan. She's mighty welcome to hab it, an' so is yo' Freddie, but Dinah wants to use it a bit now."

Flossie knew nothing of the missing pan, and it was added to the other mysteries of Red Gate Farm.

The work of picking the cherries was still going on full swing, for the sooner the fruit was gotten to market the better prices the growers would get. One night Mr. Winton called on Mr. Bobbsey and asked:

"Can you lend me some of your pickers to-morrow? I need to clean up two or three big trees in a hurry and I haven't enough workers."

"I can lend you half a dozen," Mr. Bobbsey said. "I'm over my rush."

"I'd like to pick cherries for you, Mr. Winton," said Bert. "I can't do it as fast as some, but I'll try."

"Bert is a pretty good little helper," said his father. "I'll lend him to you with the others."

"I'll pay the regular prices," went on Mr. Winton, and so it was arranged.

"Don't you want to pick for Mr. Winton, too, Nan?" asked her twin.

"No," was the reply. "We're going to make cookies in the morning."

The next day Bert went to work in the orchard opposite his father's place.

"What if you meet Nick Dodge?" asked Nan, as her brother was leaving the house in the morning.

"I guess Mr. Winton will make him behave," was the answer. "Anyhow, we're even, and it wasn't my fault Nick fell in the mud hole the second time. I guess he won't do anything."

In truth, Nick did not seem inclined that way. He did not notice Bert, who reported at the Winton orchard with the other pickers, and Bert soon got over a little feeling of nervousness.

He climbed into a tree that was laden with cherries and in a short time had a big tin pail full. He took this down to the ground and was about to pick it up and carry it to the sorting shed when Nick came along carrying a ladder.

"Out of the way!" cried the peddler's boy, and the next instant he did a mean trick, for he swung his ladder about, hitting Bert's pail and sending the cherries scattering over the ground.

"Hey! Quit that!" yelled Bert, but it was too late. The damage had been done.

CHAPTER XIX

LONG TAILS

BERT BOBBSEY was so surprised by Nick's act that, after his first sudden cry, which did no good, he just stood there, staring at the overturned pail of cherries. The other boy laughed as he passed on with the ladder, muttering:

"You want to keep out of the way when I come past. I'm in a hurry. Watch out for yourself!"

It was on the tip of Bert's tongue to shout something back at Nick, and then to run after him and perhaps get into a fight with him, when another voice called:

"Wait a minute there, young man!"

Both boys turned to see Mr. Overton, one of the farm foremen, coming up through the orchard.

"Pick up those cherries and put them back in that pail!" ordered Mr. Overton, pointing a stern finger at Nick.

"They aren't my cherries!" was Nick's answer.

"I know it," went on Mr. Overton. "They belong to this boy. Your name is Bobbsey, isn't it?"

"Yes, sir," answered Bert.

"Well, you pick them up, Nick. You spilled them and you are going to pick them up."

"He got in my way and this ladder hit his pail!" blustered Nick. "I didn't do it on purpose.

"Yes, you did!" declared the foreman. "I was watching and I saw you deliberately go out of your way to bang that ladder against this Bobbsey boy's pail and knock it over. It was a mean trick, and if you try any more like it you'll lose your job around here! Now pick up those cherries before I call Mr. Winton!"

Bert was glad enough to keep still now and allow the foreman to make matters right. He knew Nick had done the trick on purpose.

"Come on now!" ordered Mr. Overton sharply, as Nick stood there. "Put that ladder down and pick up those cherries!"

"Aw, what'd he want to get in my way for?" growled Nick. "I couldn't help banging his pail."

"I know better than that, and so do you," was the cool answer of the foreman. "No more words! Pick up those cherries!"

Nick, with a growl, put down the ladder and, getting on his hands and knees, began gathering the fruit. Luckily most of the cherries had fallen on clean grass where they came to no harm, and Bert's pail was nearly as full as at first when Nick's task was completed.

"Take them to the ticket shed now, you Bobbsey," suggested the foreman. "And if this lad bothers you again let me know."

"All right," was Bert's reply.

"But I don't believe he will," went on the foreman. "If he does, he'll be out of a job."

To this Nick did not answer, but there was an ugly look on his face as he walked on with the ladder, and Bert felt that the other lad would make trouble for him if he could.

Nick was not seen again that day in the part of the orchard where Bert was put to work. Probably he was sent to pick in another section so he would not have a chance to play more tricks.

As for Bert, he worked hard picking cherries. Now that he had earned enough in his father's orchard to buy himself a new fishing rod, he had made up his mind to buy a new reel as well, in order to wind up his line when he caught a fish.

When he was smaller, any sort of a pole and line did for Bert. He did not bother with a reel to take up his line. When he got a bite he just pulled the fish up out of the water with a sudden jerk.

"But I'm going to be a regular fisherman when I grow up," Bert told Nan that evening; "and regular fishermen have reels. So I'll get me a new one."

"I'll come over and help you pick cherries in Mr. Winton's orchard if you want me to," Bert's sister offered.

"Thanks, but I guess you'd better not," Bert decided. "There are a lot of rough boys there besides Nick, and they might make trouble. I can pick enough by myself to get money for a reel."

In spite of what Mr. Overton had said to Nick about discharging that lad if he played any more tricks, Bert was on the lookout for trouble, and when he had his pail or basket filled with cherries he took care that the peddler's boy was not around when it was carried to the shed.

One afternoon, two days after he had started to work in the Winton orchard, Bert was on his way back to Red Gate Farm when he heard, down in a grassy lane that extended out to the main road, the voices of Flossie and Freddie in dispute.

"I'm going to take the money!" Freddie was saying.

"No! I am!" declared Flossie. "I made the most juice, and I'm going to take the money!"

"The man always takes in the money!" insisted her brother. "You can fill the glasses!"

"I wonder what those two tykes are up to now," thought Bert, with a smile.

As he walked on, hurrying to get past a

clump of bushes at the road end of the lane, he heard a startled cry and then Freddie cried:

"There! Now see what you did! You upset everything!"

"You did it yourself!" wailed Flossie.

It was plain that both children were crying, and a moment later the two small Bobbsey twins came running out to the road and Bert was much surprised when he saw their faces covered with red spots and streaks.

"They must have fallen down and cut themselves!" he thought as he ran forward, crying: "What's the matter, Freddie? Are you hurt, Flossie? What happened?"

"He wouldn't let me take in the money!" sobbed the little girl.

"I wanted her to dish out the juice!" was Freddie's answer.

"The way you look you both need a doctor!" exclaimed Bert, and he was afraid the children had been badly cut in a fall. But when he got close to them he saw that they were covered with red cherry juice.

Then he looked down the lane and saw where the two had set up a little roadside stand, such as children sometimes erect for the sale of lemonade. But in the case of Flossie and Freddie the stand was upset in place of being set up. A pitcher and some glasses were scattered about, while red cherry juice was splattered everywhere. It was some of this juice that had gotten on the faces of the younger twins.

"Now keep still and tell me all about it," said Bert, when he found out the two were not hurt. Wetting his handkerchief in a little brook that ran at the side of the road, he washed the faces of his brother and sister.

"We squeezed out a lot of cherry juice," explained Freddie, "and Mother said we could sell it out at the road, if anybody wanted to stop and buy it. But Flossie wouldn't!"

"What wouldn't she do?" asked Bert.

"She wouldn't dish out the juice and let me take in the money," went on Freddie. "I would have given her half, anyhow."

"I wanted to take in the money, and he wouldn't let me," declared Flossie. "So I said I wouldn't play and——"

"Then she got up to go home," Freddie

took up the story, "and I grabbed hold of her dress, and she pulled away and—and——"

"The stand upset and I got all the cherry juice!" wailed Flossie.

"Well, never mind!" consoled Bert. "You aren't hurt, and I guess the juice won't do your clothes any harm. I got most of it off your faces," he added with a laugh, as he looked at his stained and wet handkerchief. "And, anyhow, I don't believe many people would stop and buy cherry juice when there are so many cherries to be had for the asking around here."

"Well, anyhow, we haven't any juice to sell now, 'cause it's all spilled," sighed Freddie.

So ended the venture which the small twins made into trade. Their mother had not thought they would sell much cherry juice when they begged for permission to set up a new kind of lemonade stand, but she did not want to disappoint them, so she let them try.

They had got some partly crushed cherries from the sorting shed and Dinah gave them a potato masher with which they crushed out more juice, straining it through a sieve. Then they put it into a pitcher, and with glasses arranged their stand.

"They certainly were a queer-looking sight when I met them!" chuckled Bert, after he had led the two little ones home.

"Anyhow, I didn't mean to help Flossie upset the stand," said Freddie. "And she can play with my fire engine if she wants to."

"And you can hold my best doll if you like," added Flossie.

Freddie was quite a little man and too polite to say that he did not care for dolls, which he did not. Nor did Flossie take much interest in the fire engine, though she did not say so to her twin, keeping such an opinion for Nan's ears.

The excitement over the upset cherry-juice stand was forgotten the next morning when, as Daddy Bobbsey was on his way to take the train for Lakeport, where he had to go to attend to some business, he called out into the hall:

"Has any one taken my knife?"

"Your knife? Why, no!" answered his wife. "Where did you have it last?"

"I laid it out on my bureau so I wouldn't forget to take it this morning," said Mr. Bobbsey. "But now it is gone. Did you take it, Bert?"

"No, Dad," was the answer. "I have a knife of my own."

"How about you, Nan?"

"I didn't touch it, nor even see it, Daddy."

Neither Flossie nor Freddie had seen their father's knife, and as Mr. Bobbsey was sure he had left it on the bureau his wife said:

"It was taken just as Bert's watch was, and my cameo pin. I really think something must be done about this."

"It's that Nick Dodge!" declared Bert.

"We can't be sure about that," replied his father. "Wait until I get back and I'll look into this. Too many things are being missed around here. If Nick—or any other of the strange cherry pickers—is to blame, we must put a stop to it."

Then Mr. Bobbsey hurried for his train, and Bert went over to the other farm to pick more cherries, for those remaining on the trees at Red Gate would not be ready to gather for a few more days.

It was when he was on his way home to lunch, taking a short cut through a little patch of woods, that Bert met his sister Nan. She had been to the store in the village for Dinah, and when Bert saw her she was running fast.

"What's your hurry?" he asked. "It's too hot to run."

"Oh, Bert, I'm so frightened!" gasped Nan, turning toward him.

"Frightened?" he exclaimed. "Has that Nick Dodge been teasing you? If he has——"

"No, it wasn't Nick!" gasped Nan. "Oh, Bert, it's an animal with a long tail—two or three animals—back there in the woods!"

"What kind of animals?" cried Bert.

"All I could see was their tails!" panted Nan. "Such long tails as they had—all curly and covered with hair! Oh, Bert, I'm so frightened!"

CHAPTER XX

WHAT NAN SAW

"Now look here, Nan!" exclaimed Bert, and he took hold of his sister's arm. "There's no use of being frightened just because you saw what you think was an animal's tail."

"I didn't think it—I know it!" insisted Nan. "And there was more than one. I dropped the bag of sugar, I was so scared."

"What bag of sugar?"

"The one I went to the store to get for Dinah."

"Come on back and show me where you saw those tails," suggested Bert, with a laugh. "I guess you'll find out it was only some dangling wild grape vines swinging in the wind."

"Do you think so?" and Nan was calmer now.

"I'm pretty sure it was," went on her brother. "There aren't any animals with long tails in these woods. It was just swinging vines."

"Well, maybe it was," admitted Nan. "But I surely thought they were tails. And when I heard them chatter——"

"Chatter!" cried Bert. "Do you mean the tails chattered?"

"No! But the animals the tails belong to chattered and yelled," went on Nan. "I'm sure I heard them."

"I guess you must have fallen asleep and dreamed it all," said Bert, looking curiously at his sister. "Come on back and show me."

"Oh, Bert, I don't want to! I'm afraid!"

"Come on! There's nothing to be afraid of. We have to get the bag of sugar you dropped, anyhow!"

"Yes, I suppose so," agreed Nan. "But you go ahead. I don't want to see those tails again, nor hear the chattering."

"I guess what you thought was chattering was the wind blowing through a hollow tree!" chuckled Bert. "And the tails were vines, I'm sure. It would be great, though, if there were some wild animals in these woods."

"Great!" cried Nan. "I call it terrible!"

After a little more talk she told where she had dropped the bag of sugar, to begin running home, and Bert finally persuaded her to walk along behind him and point out the place.

As the two older Bobbsey twins neared the spot Nan looked anxiously around. Finally close to a dense thicket of bushes on one side of the path through the clump of trees, the girl pointed to a large rock and said:

"I dropped the bag of sugar there!"

"You couldn't have!" retorted her brother. "It isn't there now."

"The bag is," said Nan, taking another look, "but there isn't any sugar in it. See? It's empty!"

"So it is!" agreed Bert who, now that he was a little closer, could see the crumpled bag. All too plain, it was empty. The sugar had been taken out, but little heaps of white grains here and there on or near the path showed what had happened.

"The long-tails took the sugar!" exclaimed

Nan in a whisper. "Oh, Bert, let's not stay here!"

"Wait a minute!" he said. "I want to find out more about this. If there are wild animals with long tails who eat sugar in these woods, Dad and the other farmers will want to know about them. I'm going to take another look!"

"Don't leave me, Bert!" begged Nan, as the boy moved farther along on the path.

"Then come on up closer," he suggested. "I can't see from here. There's nothing to be afraid of!"

Truly, there did not seem to be. The woods were very quiet, save for the rustling of leaves in the wind, and the sun was shining brightly outside of the little grove.

But suddenly, as Nan and Bert moved closer to that empty sugar bag, the girl grasped her brother's arm and, pointing upward into a tree, whispered:

"There's one now!"

"One what?" asked Bert.

"One of the long-tails. And there's another! And another! Oh, Bert! There's a whole lot of 'em! Why, Bert! They're *monkeys!* They're long-tailed *monkeys!*"

At that instant Bert also saw them—a group of monkeys huddled in a heap on the branch of a tree over the heads of the boy and girl. Monkeys with their long tails either clutching the limb or switching from side to side.

"Monkeys! Monkeys!" murmured Bert, hardly able to believe what his eyes saw. "How did they get here?"

Nan did not answer. She was watching one of the larger of the long-tailed animals, and saw it licking its forepaws.

"Look, Bert!" his sister whispered. "He must be one of those who took the sugar out of the bag after I dropped it! His paws are all sticky!"

"So they are!" Bert agreed. "There's another licking his paws, too, Nan! They took your sugar, all right!"

"But where did the monkeys come from?" Nan wanted to know, while she and Bert continued to gaze up into the tree at the long-tailed band. "And what a lot of them there are. One, two, three—" she lost count because the monkeys began moving about, but Bert said:

"There must be a dozen of them!"

Then, as if they did not like to be talked about, the monkeys began chattering, screaming, and scolding in high voices.

"There!" cried Nan. "That's what I heard before. And I did see their long tails Bert!"

"Yes, I guess you did, and it must have been kind of scary when you didn't know what they were," the Bobbsey lad was forced to admit. "I thought you imagined it all. Whew! This is great!"

Nan was not frightened now. She was just curious, as was Bert, as to how the monkeys could have got to the woods.

"Look out, Bert!" suddenly cried Nan. "They're coming down! They're going to chase us!"

Whether this was so or not the two Bobbsey twins did not stop to see. Certainly some of the monkeys began swinging down from the upper branches of the tree, and a few of them appeared to be coming in the direction of the boy and girl. They kept up a shrill chattering and shrieking and though Bert and his twin were not cowards, they had read enough about big and little apes to know that an angry one can do a great deal of harm.

"Come on!" Bert cried, seizing Nan's hand. "We'll go and tell Dad about these monkeys. He'll know what to do."

"Dad has gone to the city," explained Nan.

"Well, then, we'll tell Mother and Mr. Winton and Mr. Tansy. These monkeys ought to be caught. They may pick all the rest of the cherries!"

But for the present it seemed to be the children who were likely to be caught by the long-tailed animals, and not the monkeys by their human enemies. For the whole troupe made a sudden dash at Nan and Bert and the boy and girl ran as fast as they could to get into the open.

Very likely the monkeys were only going to a new place to perch, and were not thinking of chasing Nan and Bert, for they did not follow the children more than a few feet. Then, up into other trees the long-tailed beasts swung themselves with more chattering and scoldings.

But Nan and Bert did not think it safe to linger, and ran on, not stopping until they reached home, where their mother, who was on the porch, saw them coming and wondered at their haste.

"Strange news, children! Strange news!" she called to them, waving in one hand a newspaper, a weekly one published in a town not far from Cherry Corners. "The *Gazette* has just come, my dears," said Mrs. Bobbsey, "and it tells about a lot of monkeys that escaped from the circus train which went through here the other day. Just think of it—eighteen monkeys, fresh from the jungle, escaped from the circus train! Isn't that great news?"

"We have stranger news than that!" cried Bert.

"You have? What is it?" asked his mother.

"Nan and I saw those monkeys! They're in the oak grove down by the brook! Eighteen monkeys with long tails!"

CHAPTER XXI

FREDDIE'S ENGINE

MRS. BOBBSEY did not know for a moment whether or not to take seriously what Bert said. He seemed to be laughing and was much excited, and he often played jokes. But Nan joined in.

"Yes, Mother! I saw the monkeys first! They frightened me and I ran and dropped the bag of sugar. Then I met Bert and we went back to look, and the monkeys had taken all the sugar out of the bag and were up in a tree! You ought to see them!"

"Really?" asked Mrs. Bobbsey.

"Real monkeys!" exclaimed Bert. "We didn't know where they were from, but if they got out of the circus train there will be a reward for telling about them or getting them back. I'm going to do it!"

"Wait a minute now, Bert," advised his mother. "Tell me more about this."

This he and Nan did by turns. Then Mrs. Bobbsey read from the weekly paper the account of the monkeys getting away from the circus train.

It appeared that when the circus reached the town for which it was headed when passing through Cherry Corners, it was discovered that about eighteen monkeys, most of them captives fresh from the jungle, had gotten out of their traveling cage, and none of the circus men knew where they were. The beasts, it was said in the paper, were not dangerous unless some one tried to harm them.

"But they are very mischievous," the paper said, "and will pick up little things, especially if they are bright in color. So if any near-by residents miss looking glasses or silver knives or forks, they may guess that some of these escaped monkeys are in their vicinity. Unless it can be proved that human hands had to do with the disappearance of the trinkets."

"That's it!" cried Bert, excitedly jumping about. "That's it!"

"What's what?" asked his mother, smiling at his eagerness.

"That's what has been happening to the things that have been missing from around here," Bert went on. "Those monkeys have been coming in windows at night and taking everything they could lay their hands on."

"Monkeys haven't hands," Nan declared to her brother.

"Well, paws, then."

"But monkeys do have hands. Men and the apes have hands and not paws," Mrs. Bobbsey told the twins.

"It's all the same. I wonder if they took my watch?" cried Bert excitedly.

"If they did, then Nick didn't do it," Nan remarked.

"No, I guess he didn't," Bert answered. "Isn't it queer? Who would ever think of a troupe of monkeys escaping from a circus train and hiding in the woods around here to take things!"

Flossie and Freddie came along just then, and, hearing some of what was said, asked to be told the whole story, which was related to them.

"If the monkeys take any of my dolls, I'll chase after them!" threatened Flossie.

"So will I, if they take my toy fire engine!" declared Freddie. "And I'll pull their long tails!"

"Now see here!" exclaimed their mother, seriously. "I don't want you twins to start any monkey hunts by yourselves. Remember that, Flossie and Freddie!" and she shook a finger at each of them in turn.

"May I hunt the monkeys?" asked Bert.

"Not unless your father says so," answered his mother. "Even though monkeys are funny to look at, they may bite or scratch if you try to catch them. Wait until your father comes home and we will tell him all about these escaped monkeys."

"Don't you think, Mother," asked Bert, "that we had better tell Mr. Tansy and the other farmers now? Maybe they might want to try to catch the monkeys. The monkeys might spoil a lot of cherries."

"That's so," agreed Mrs. Bobbsey. "Well, then, Bert, you and Nan may spread the news."

After lunch Bert went back to his work of

picking cherries, and the news he brought with him caused a stir. It spread from one farm to another, and several of the men engaged in picking cherries gave up their jobs and started off for the woods, saying they were going to try to capture a monkey or two and get the reward they were sure the circus people would offer.

There was much talk as to how the monkeys could have gotten out of their car, but no one knew for certain.

When Bert was on his way home that evening, after his day in the cherry orchard, he met some of the men who had gone to the woods to hunt monkeys.

"Did you catch any?" he asked.

"Not a one!" was the answer of a big, good-natured man. "I guess the monkeys got word we were coming and they hid."

"But they're in the woods all right," said another man. "We saw several farmers who'd caught sight of them."

Bert said that if the monkeys had escaped when the circus train passed through Cherry Corners some days ago, it was queer they had only showed themselves now, when Nan first caught sight of them.

"I guess they hid in the woods, afraid to come out, after they escaped from the circus car," said the big man. "When they got hungry, though, they began showing themselves. I guess the sugar your sister dropped was just what they wanted."

Bert agreed this might be so, and hurried home to see if his father had arrived, as Bert wanted permission to hunt the long-tailed creatures.

Mr. Bobbsey's train was not yet in, but would come soon. Meanwhile, Mrs. Bobbsey, the children, and Dinah talked about the monkeys that, it was thought, were roaming the woods in the neighborhood of Cherry Corners.

"It mus' 'a' been dem long-tailed chaps whut done tuck mah shiny pans!" declared Dinah.

"And maybe they took my cake, and Nick didn't at all!" added Nan.

"That's so," admitted Bert. "I didn't think of that! All the while I was sure Nick did it."

"And it was a monkey that came into my room that night!" exclaimed Freddie.

"I believe it was!" said his mother.

"And in mine, too!" went on Flossie.

"Did it look like a monkey?" asked Nan.

"I don't zackly remember, but it had a long tail," said the little girl.

It was surmised by more than Freddie and Flossie that one or more of the circus animals had entered the Bobbsey house, not only in the night when Flossie and Freddie saw them, but several other times, when things were taken.

"Then a monkey must have my knife!" said Mr. Bobbsey when he reached home a little later in the evening and heard the story. "This is great news. Wild monkeys in cherry land!" and he laughed as he pretended to wrestle with Freddie.

"Can we hunt them?" asked Bert eagerly. "If we could catch them we'd get a big reward from the circus."

"Maybe and maybe not," laughed Mr. Bobbsey. "I guess the circus people would be glad to pay a reward, for monkeys are valuable animals. But it isn't so easy to catch them. However, we'll see about it."

Mr. Bobbsey talked with his farmer neighbors, and they all agreed that something ought to be done, not because the monkeys were dangerous, but that they were mischievous. That night Flossie and Freddie hardly wanted to go to bed, fearing one of the long-tailed creatures might again come in the window.

But their mother pointed out to them that now their windows had wire screens in, which was not the case before, and no monkeys could get in. This satisfied the small twins, and at last they fell asleep.

Bert and some of the other boy cherry pickers were on the lookout until it was time for them to go to bed, but they neither saw nor heard anything of the monkeys.

The next day, when Bert had gone to pick cherries in his father's orchard, for now the last of the crop at Red Gate Farm was being gathered, something happened in Dinah's kitchen.

Bert had come to the house for a drink of water, after spending some time up in a tree, when he heard Dinah shouting:

"Get out! Get out mah kitchen, yo' long-tailed imp!"

Then followed a shrill chattering and the sound of blows.

"Dinah's caught a monkey!" cried Freddie, who was playing in the yard with his toy fire engine. "Dinah's caught a monkey!"

Much excited, he and Bert, followed by Flossie and Nan, ran to the rear of the house. They saw a curious sight. Perched on the window sill of the kitchen was a large monkey, but it did not seem to be running away. In fact, it could not. Something was holding it fast.

"Dinah's got him by the tail!" yelled Bert, with a laugh.

That is just what had happened. The black cook had surprised a monkey in her kitchen in the act of taking a cake off the table. She rushed at the animal, at the same time banging two empty pans together and shouting an alarm. The monkey chattered back. Then the fat cook made a jump and caught hold of the monkey's tail as it leaped for the open window.

"Get out ob mah kitchen!" yelled Dinah.

but the poor monkey could not while she had hold of its tail.

At last, however, the monkey pulled loose, and with a final scream and chatter of rage and pain, climbed up into a tree, clutching in one hand the remains of the crushed cake.

"Whar am de police?" cried Dinah. "Get me a policeman, honey lambs!" she begged the four twins. "I done wants dat monkey arrested!"

But Bert, Nan, and the others were laughing so hard they could not have called a policeman had there been one in Cherry Corners.

"The beasts are certainly getting very bold!" declared Mrs. Bobbsey when, in answer to the shouts of excitement and laughter, she arrived on the scene. "I think your father will have to notify the circus people to come and get their jungle beasts."

"Maybe the whole circus will come here," said Flossie, with a laugh.

Mrs. Bobbsey and the older twins went around to the front yard, leaving Dinah bemoaning her lost cake. Then a sudden cry of dismay arose from Freddie.

"Maybe a monkey has him!" shouted Nan, starting on a run, followed by Bert and his mother. But Freddie's voice came back to them as he cried:

"My engine's gone! My toy fire engine! I just saw a monkey take it! Oh, he's got my engine!"

Bert and Nan ran around the corner of the house just in time to see one of the long-tailed apes scampering up a tree with Freddie's beloved toy.

CHAPTER XXII

CATCHING THE MONKEYS

"GIVE me my engine! Come back with my engine!" cried Freddie, as he ran to the foot of the tree up which the monkey had scrambled. "Bert! Make him give me back my engine!"

Glad as Bert would have been to do this, it was impossible, for the monkey moved too quickly. Like a streak of brown light he scampered up the tree, and only by the movement of the limbs and branches could it be told that he was there For he could not be seen.

"They are getting very bold!" declared Mrs. Bobbsey. "Nothing will be safe from the little rascals."

"Maybe Bert can climb up that tree and get Freddie's engine back," suggested Nan.

"Oh, yes, please do!" begged the little fellow.

"You'll need one of the cherry ladders, though," went on Nan. The tree had no branches low down that Bert might have grasped. But the monkey, carrying Freddie's engine, had no trouble in climbing it.

"It wouldn't do any good to get a ladder," said Bert, who had been walking around the tree, looking up into the branches.

"Why not?" Freddie wanted to know.

"Because the monkey with your engine isn't up in this tree any more," went on Bert. "Look—he just jumped into that other tree, and there he goes, off to the woods!"

It was true enough. Just as he had traveled in his native jungle, through the tops of the trees, the monkey was now leaping from branch to branch in the trees of Red Gate Farm. There was a line of them extending down the road, and so close that their branches touched and interlaced. It was easy for a monkey to leap from one branch to another and from one tree into the next one. In this way the little beast could travel along, without touching the ground, until he reached the woods.

"How am I going to get my engine back?" wailed Freddie. "If I had a gun I'd shoot that monkey!"

"Oh, you wouldn't do that, would you, little fireman?" asked Nan. "The monkeys are so cute!"

"How can I be a fireman if I haven't my engine?" demanded Freddie. "Yes, if I had a gun I'd shoot that monkey."

"He means only shoot him a little to make him drop the engine, don't you, Freddie?" asked Flossie.

"Yes, I'd shoot him just a little," agreed her twin brother.

"Something must be done," decided Mrs. Bobbsey. "When I get a chance to talk to your father I'll ask him about it. We can't have the monkeys taking things like this all the while."

Mr. Bobbsey was seeing to the picking of the last batch of cherries, and when he came to the house to lunch his wife told him what had happened last—the taking of Freddie's engine.

"I will send a telegram to the circus people," decided Mr. Bobbsey. "I will tell them to come and catch their monkeys and take them away. We don't want them around here, though I must say they have not taken any of my cherries."

The children's father sent off a message to the circus, and then every one waited for the arrival of some animal man from the show, who would know how to secure the monkeys. Some of the men and boys on the various farms had set traps to catch the apes, but nothing had come of it.

Meanwhile, the monkeys kept coming and going. Now only one or two would be seen, swinging in the trees close to the home of the Bobbseys or on the other three farms near by. But the beasts would soon go away, perhaps not being able to get any more of Dinah's kitchen things or Nan's cakes.

Once or twice reports came from neighboring farmers' wives that their kitchens had been entered while they were out and food or bright pans taken. One boy, coming home through the woods late at night, declared a monkey swung down by its tail from a high branch and snatched off his hat. But as he did not see the beast, it was thought perhaps a low swinging branch had caught the cap, and that the boy had imagined the rest.

The cherry picking went on, Bert doing his share and earning more than enough money for his new reel as well as for his rod.

"But I'm not going to buy it until the monkeys are caught," he said. "A new, shiny reel would be just what they would pick up."

"Like my engine," sighed Freddie.

"Yes, like your engine," agreed Bert.

"I guess I'll never see it again," went on the little fellow sadly.

"No more than I will my watch or Dad his knife or Mother her cameo pin," said Bert.

The next day one of the men from the circus arrived. On reaching Cherry Corners he asked for Mr. Bobbsey and was directed to Red Gate Farm.

"I guess you have some of our monkeys here," said the circus man, with a smile. He gave his name as Mr. Dalton.

"They're around here, but we haven't any

of them," answered Mr. Bobbsey. "The trouble is we can't catch any of them, and we'd like to, for they have been causing a lot of trouble. We have set traps for them, but haven't caught any."

"It's quite a trick to catch a monkey," said Mr. Dalton. "They won't enter an ordinary trap. I have brought with me some special kinds, and we'll set them as the natives do in the jungle."

"May we see how it's done?" asked Bert.

"Well, if you stay near the traps after they're set you may scare the monkeys," the circus man said. "But after the apes are caught you may see how it is done."

"Does it hurt them?" asked Nan.

"Not a bit," was the reply.

"How did they manage to escape?" asked Mrs. Bobbsey.

"The beasts got out soon after our circus train passed through here," answered Mr. Dalton. "The monkeys were all in one car, but these which escaped, and which were rather wild, were all in one end of the car."

"What kind of a car was it?" asked Bert, with a look at Nan.

"It was a regular circus car."

"Yes, I know," went on Bert. "But did it have any kind of special pictures or looking glasses on it?"

"Oh, I see what you mean!" exclaimed Mr. Dalton. "Yes, the monkey car had pictures of lions painted on it. It wasn't a regular monkey car, but we had so many extra specimens of the long-tailed beasts that we had to use an empty lion car to move them in."

"Then Nick Dodge let the monkeys loose!" declared Bert. "For the car he climbed up on had pictures of lions on it! And he opened one of the iron-barred windows!"

"What's this?" cried the circus man in surprise.

"That's right!" chimed in Nan, and she added her story to the one her brother told, how Nick, to be smart and show off, had climbed on the circus train when it stopped for water.

"He did something to one of the windows, and a bar came loose," went on Bert. "One of the fellows said the car had monkeys in, and we saw something hairy and fuzzy at the window. Then when the train started Nick jumped off."

"And after it started, when the window was open, the train stopped again a little farther down the track, so the second engine could get water," said Nan.

"That's just about how it happened," agreed Mr. Dalton. "When the train stopped a second time the monkeys, finding the window open, either by that boy's trick or by his meddling, got out. Well, now I'll have to catch them. I'm sorry they caused you so much trouble."

"Will you get my engine back?" asked Freddie.

"I'll try, little man," was the answer.

"I'd like to get my watch," sighed Bert.

"I guess my cake is all eaten up by this time," remarked Nan, with a laugh.

"You can't tell what monkeys will do with things they take," declared the circus man. "Of course they would eat the cake. But anything bright or shiny they may carry off and hide, or they may drop it soon after picking it up. They are very curious, and it is because of that curiosity that I hope to catch them."

He had brought with him a large trunk, which was sent up from the railroad station, and this trunk, on being opened, proved to contain a number of earthen jars and some nuts.

"Monkeys are very fond of these nuts," explained Mr. Dalton. "What I am going to do is to fill these jars with nuts and set them in the woods at the place where the monkeys have been most often seen."

"Oh, you're going to feed them nuts?" asked Bert.

"Not quite," was the laughing answer. "You see the monkeys will smell or see the nuts in the jars. They will come down out of the trees to get some, and to do that they will have to thrust their paws down inside the jars. A monkey is very greedy as well as very curious. Once he has his paw inside the jar he will grasp it full of nuts. Now the openings of the jars are very small, as you see. The openings are just large enough for a monkey to slip his paw in when it is unclasped, or open. But once the monkey's paw is filled with nuts and swelled out, he cannot pull it out of the jar, and thus he is caught. With the heavy jar on his paw he can't run far and can't climb a tree, and we shall soon catch them."

"But maybe some of the stronger monkeys could run off with a jar," said Mrs. Bobbsey.

"I should have told you," added the circus man, "that we will tie the jars to trees with strong ropes."

"But if a monkey opened his fingers and lets go of the nuts that he's grabbed, his hand would be small enough then to pull it out of the jar," said Nan.

"Ah, that's just it, little girl!" exclaimed Mr. Dalton. "The monkey is so greedy that he will not let go of the nuts he has once grasped, and in that way we catch them. You will soon see."

That evening the jars were baited with the nuts and placed in the grove where the long-tailed beasts were most often seen. Word was then sent around to the different farms for the cherry pickers to keep away from the traps so the circus animals would suspect nothing.

Then followed a night of waiting, while little was talked of in the Bobbsey home but the chances of catching the nimble chaps and getting back some of the stolen things. Mr. Dalton was invited to remain as a guest at Red Gate Farm, and before Flossie and Freddie went to bed he told them many circus stories.

Early the next morning the Bobbsey twins were up and ready to go to the "monkey grove," as they called it. Mr. Bobbsey and the circus man also went, as did a number of the cherry pickers from the different farms.

Even before the grove was reached a shrill chattering and shrieking could be heard, and Mr. Dalton said:

"We've caught some monkeys, all right. I thought my traps would work!"

They had. For on arriving at the scene a curious sight met the eyes of Bert and his sisters and brother.

CHAPTER XXIII

IN THE OLD TREE

SEATED on the ground, sadly looking at their paws caught in the small openings of the jars, or trying to pull away, which they could not do on account of the jars being tied to trees, were about a dozen monkeys. They were chattering and screaming. It sounded like scolding, the Bobbsey twins thought. But almost the whole band of long-tailed apes had been caught by the circus man's trap, or rather, traps, for he had set out about twenty jars, baited with the nuts.

In the night the monkeys had gathered in the grove. They had climbed down the trees when all was quiet, and eager to get the nuts, as well as curious to see what was in the jars, they had thrust in their paws.

Greedily, they had grasped as many nuts as their fingers would hold.

"And then," said Mr. Dalton, as he stood looking at the howling, struggling monkeys, "they were caught. They didn't know enough to let go the nuts. If they had, they could have gotten away."

"How are you going to make them let go now?" asked Bert.

"Some will drop the nuts as soon as we tie them up with ropes, ready to be put back in some small cages I brought with me," said the circus man. "In other cases we may have to break the jars to make the monkey understand that he must open his fingers. But the jars are made of clay and crack easily. The monkeys will not be harmed."

At the sight of the Bobbsey twins and others who came to see how the traps had worked, the monkeys became very much excited. They tried harder than ever to get away, but they simply would not let go the nuts inside the jars, and so they were held captives by their own greed and curiosity.

Mr. Dalton knew how to handle monkeys, and he soon had the twelve bound with ropes, freed from the jars by one way or the other, and ready to be put into cages.

"How many escaped from the circus car?" asked someone.

"Eighteen in all," was the answer. "If the other six are around here I'll get them to-night."

"See if any of 'em has my fire engine!" begged Freddie. But it was plain that none of the captured monkeys had the toy. Nor did any of them have Bert's watch or Mr. Bobbsey's knife or his wife's pin.

"The things may be hidden around here in the woods," suggested Mr. Dalton. "We'll look after I set the traps again to-night."

The monkeys were well cared for, given a good feed of the very nuts that had aided in their capture, and put in small cages to be sent on to the circus.

"Did yo' all find any ob mah pans?" asked Dinah, when the children returned to breakfast.

"No. But maybe the monkeys we're going to catch to-night will have them," said Bert.

During the cherry picking that day little

was talked of save the catching of the monkeys, and what would happen by next morning was eagerly discussed.

Again the jar traps and nuts were successful, and five more of the long-tailed animals were prisoners the next morning, chattering and scolding over their plight.

"Well, I have seventeen out of the eighteen. I guess I won't bother about the other one," said the circus man, as he made ready to ship his beasts on and return to his show.

"And now we won't have to worry about things being taken," said Bert. "I guess we were wrong in thinking Nick took things."

"He may have heard that we suspected him," said Mrs. Bobbsey. "Perhaps it would be well to say we know now he had nothing to do with it."

But they did not get this chance, for Nick left his place when the circus man arrived. Perhaps the boy feared he might be arrested for having let the monkeys escape, though he really, it may be, did not intend to do so. At any rate, he left Cherry Corners in a hurry.

The last of the cherries were almost picked

and Bert decided that he could take a day off and look for some of the things the monkeys had taken. He and Nan went to the grove where the traps had been set, and, after looking around and poking in holes and in hollow stumps, they found Freddie's toy engine. It was down in a hole almost covered with leaves.

"Freddie will be glad to get this back," said Bert, noting that the toy had suffered little harm. The rubber hose was missing, a monkey probably having pulled that loose. Or perhaps there was a dispute between two of the beasts over the plaything.

"I guess it was too heavy for them to carry around," suggested Nan, as she and her brother hastened home with the recovered toy, which Freddie was delighted to get back.

"I won't shoot any monkeys now!" he said.

Though Nan and Bert searched during the next two days, they found no trace of the silver watch, their mother's cameo pin, nor of their father's knife. However, some of Dinah's pans were discovered in the weeds at the end of the garden, where the monkeys had dropped them. And other things, taken from the farms near by, were found in various places.

The missing eighteenth monkey was not found, and what became of him was never learned by the Bobbsey twins.

The last of the cherry crop had been shipped away, and Mrs. Bobbsey and Dinah had canned enough of the fruit to last all winter.

"We have finished just about in time, too," said Mr. Bobbsey on the night when the last of the fruit had been gathered and the pickers had left.

"Why?" asked Bert.

"Because I think we are going to have a bad storm. The weather has been very good so far, but now we are going to have some of the other sort."

So it proved, for in the middle of the night the wind began to howl and the rain began to fall, so that when the Bobbsey twins awakened in the morning they looked out on a water-swept and wind-lashed orchard and farm.

"We couldn't pick cherries to-day if we wanted to, and it's a good thing we don't," said Mr. Bobbsey. "We shall soon be going back home now."

"Then we want to have some fun!" exclaimed Bert.

"Let's play up in the attic!" suggested Nan, and the four had a jolly time dressing up in the soldier uniform and playing with the other things found there.

Just before noon the storm grew worse. The wind blew a gale, and suddenly a loud crash sounded outside the rear of the house.

"What was that?" cried Nan.

Bert ran to the attic window and looked out.

"It's the big cherry tree!" he cried. "It's blown down!"

"Oh, let's go out and see it!" cried Flossie and Freddie.

However, their mother would not allow this until after the storm had ceased. It showed signs of slackening in the middle of the afternoon, and then the children, with their father and mother, went out to look at the fallen tree.

"It was very old, hollow, and rotten," said Mr. Bobbsey as they walked toward it, with Snap barking and leaping about. "The old tree has given us its last cherries."

The Bobbseys gathered about the fallen trunk, which had broken off about three feet from the ground, leaving a jagged, hollow stump sticking up. Bert leaned over and looked down into the hollow. Then he gave a startled cry.

"What is it?" Nan asked. "The missing monkey?"

"No," answered Bert. "But my missing watch and Mother's missing pin. Here they are, in this old hollow tree!"

"The monkeys must have stuffed them into a hole in the trunk and they fell to the bottom and have been here ever since," said Mrs. Bobbsey, as she took her pin from Bert. It had been kept dry in the deep hollow cherry tree, as had Bert's watch, and neither was harmed.

"See if my knife is there," suggested Mr. Bobbsey. But that was not to be found. However, as Nan said, they were lucky to get back the watch and the pin.

"And I got my fire engine!" shouted Freddie, as if that were all that mattered.

"Well, the monkeys made a lot of fun while they were here," remarked Bert, as he put his watch in his pocket.

With Mrs. Bobbsey wearing her cameo pin, the family went back to the house. The falling tree had done no harm.

The storm was soon over, and after a few more happy days on Red Gate Farm at Cherry Corners, the Bobbsey twins started back to Lakeport.

"I wonder what will happen next!" exclaimed Nan excitedly.

"I don't know," answered Bert. "But I hope we come cherry picking again next summer."

What was to happen to him and his brother and sisters was far different but just as much fun. The story is called "The Bobbsey Twins and Their Schoolmates."

Before this, however, they were to return home and get acquainted again with their pets and the little friends with whom they loved to play.

THE END